## "I saw you walking on the grounds earlier, Signorina."

Max's accented English delivered in a deep masculine voice vibrated to her insides. Its cadence sent a delicious tremor through her system even though the night was warm. "I hoped you would come to the pool. Swim with me."

His ardent demand was whispered with a pulsating urgency that said his life wouldn't be worth living if she didn't consent.

"I'm not wearing a swimsuit."

"Does it matter?" came the breathtaking question.

With great daring, Greer slipped off her gold sandals, left her gold watch and gold lamé clutch bag on a table near the deep end of the pool, then dove in headfirst—still fully clothed!

Dear Reader,

I came from a family of five sisters and one brother. The four oldest girls were my parents' first family. There was a space before my baby sister and baby brother came along.

My mother called the first four her little women, and gave each of us a Madame Alexander doll from the *Little Women* series based on the famous book by Louisa May Alcott. We may not have been quadruplets, but we were close in age and definitely felt a connection to each other that often meant we tuned into each other's thoughts as we sang, played, studied and traveled together.

In our early twenties I recall a time when I took the train from Paris, France, where I'd been studying, to meet one of my sisters at the port in Genoa, Italy, where her ship came in from New York. She was returning to school in Perugia, Italy. Some of my choicest memories are our glorious adventures as two blond American sisters on vacation along the French and Italian rivieras, dodging Mediterranean playboys.

When I conceived *The Husband Fund* trilogy for Harlequin Romance®, I have no doubt the idea of triplet sisters coming to Europe on a lark to intentionally meet some gorgeous Riviera playboys sprang to life from my own family experiences at home and abroad.

Meet Greer, Olivia and Piper, three characters drawn from my imagination who probably have traits from all four of my wonderful, intelligent, talented sisters in their makeup.

Enjoy!

Rebecca Winters

Book 2: *To Win His Heart,* Harlequin Romance #3827,
on sale January 2005
Book 3: *To Marry for Duty,* Harlequin Romance #3835,
on sale March 2005

www.rebeccawinters-author.com

# TO CATCH A GROOM

## Rebecca Winters

The
HUSBAND
F U N D

HARLEQUIN®

TORONTO • NEW YORK • LONDON
AMSTERDAM • PARIS • SYDNEY • HAMBURG
STOCKHOLM • ATHENS • TOKYO • MILAN • MADRID
PRAGUE • WARSAW • BUDAPEST • AUCKLAND

ISBN 0-373-03819-4

TO CATCH A GROOM

First North American Publication 2004.

Copyright © 2004 by Rebecca Winters.

All rights reserved. Except for use in any review, the reproduction or utilization of this work in whole or in part in any form by any electronic, mechanical or other means, now known or hereafter invented, including xerography, photocopying and recording, or in any information storage or retrieval system, is forbidden without the written permission of the publisher, Harlequin Enterprises Limited, 225 Duncan Mill Road, Don Mills, Ontario, Canada M3B 3K9.

All characters in this book have no existence outside the imagination of the author and have no relation whatsoever to anyone bearing the same name or names. They are not even distantly inspired by any individual known or unknown to the author, and all incidents are pure invention.

This edition published by arrangement with Harlequin Books S.A.

® and TM are trademarks of the publisher. Trademarks indicated with ® are registered in the United States Patent and Trademark Office, the Canadian Trade Marks Office and in other countries.

www.eHarlequin.com

Printed in U.S.A.

# CHAPTER ONE

*April 14, Kingston, New York*

GREER DUCHESS could tell by tapping feet and shifting bodies that her sisters were getting antsy. "We're almost through, guys. For November is it agreed we'll go with Ginger Rogers Did Everything Fred Astaire Did, But She Did It Backward And In High Heels?"

"Like I said before, not everyone who buys our calendars knows who Ginger Rogers is," Olivia spoke up.

"It doesn't matter, does it? Piper's drawing is so wonderful they'll still get the point," Greer murmured, making a unilateral decision on the spot. She adored the stylized cartoons of Luigio and Violetta, the two winsome Italian pigeons who were in love with each other.

Though Piper did the actual drawings, and Olivia headed sales, Greer was the instigator and power behind their business enterprise.

"Moving on, here are the choices we narrowed down for December. Behind Every Successful Man Is A Surprised Woman, and, A Man's Got To Do What A Man's Got To Do. A Woman's Got To Do What He Can't."

Piper got up and stretched her softly rounded body. "I liked both those sayings the first time you thought them up."

"I still like them," Olivia asserted. "Your clever mind never ceases to impress me, Greer. You make the decision. We trust your judgment," she said, rising to her feet on long, shapely legs. "Now we've really got to go or we'll be late for the reading of Daddy's will. We're supposed to be there at ten.''

"Okay. Get the car started while I e-mail this to Don. It'll take me two secs.''

Within a minute the sent message appeared on the computer screen. She felt relief that next year's calendar entitled, For Women Only, would be printed and ready for distribution in May which was only a few weeks away.

Don Jardine, one of several guys she and her sisters had been dating, was the owner of the print shop. He did a terrific job for them.

Unfortunately he kept hinting that he wanted her to take him seriously because he'd fallen for her. But she wasn't in love with him. Lately she'd found excuses not to go out with him anymore. If they could just remain business friends...

All things considered, Duchesse Designs—her brain child inspired by their only illustrious female ancestor and heroine—the Duchess of Parma, a woman in advance of her time—was doing much better than her initial conservative estimates indicated.

With orders from all over the country quadrupling since Christmas, she and her sisters were going to make a substantial profit. For the first time in five years they would be able to invest part of their earnings while they put the rest back into their company.

Naturally that was going to mean more money for Don and make him happy, too. Maybe happy enough to forgive her? She had yet to find that out. If he sent a reply e-mail that she'd better take her business to someone else, then she would have her answer.

After turning on the answering machine, she dashed out of the basement apartment to join her sisters.

All the rituals of laying their beloved father to rest had been observed except for this visit to Mr. Carlson's office.

It was a formality. Once it was behind them, they'd be able to channel their sorrow by expanding their growing business.

Twenty minutes later they arrived at the law firm in downtown Kingston, New York. The receptionist showed them into the conference room where a TV and DVD player had been set up.

Soon after they'd sat down, Mr. Carlson walked in with a legal file under one arm. He greeted them, shook hands, then took his place at the end of the rectangular conference table.

"Your father asked me to read you a letter he wrote in his own hand." He opened the file and drew it out. Once his bifocals were in place, he cleared his throat.

*"To my darling daughters Greer, Piper and Olivia, whom I've always referred to as my precious pigeons. You came along after I turned fifty and had despaired of ever giving your mother children—*

*"If Walter Carlson has assembled you for the reading of this will, then it means my troublesome old ticker finally gave out and you've already been informed that our humble home has to be sold to pay all the medical expenses.*

*"I wish I could have left it to you, but it wasn't meant to be. At least you aren't saddled with debts. Walt will pay the latest bills and is taking care of everything. He's aware you need time to find another place to live. Therefore he will be the one to let you know how soon you must move out.*

*"My greatest sadness is that none of you has ever shown the slightest inclination to marry. It worried your mother before she died, and it upsets me even more. I remember her last words to you: find a good man to marry right away and settle down to raise a family. My last words echo hers.*

*"To that end I'm bequeathing $5,000 to each of you.*

*It's from the Husband Fund your mother and I created before she passed away. You can spend it any way you want so long as it's used in the pursuit of a spouse to help you enjoy this life to the fullest.*

"*You will receive those checks today. For this day and age it's not much, but it's given with all my love. I know my girls will be fine because you're intelligent, talented, resourceful and have created a solid Internet business since college. However as you will discover when you put this money to the proper use, there's more to life than earning a living.*

"*To stimulate your thinking, I'm insisting you remain in Walt's office to watch your mother's favorite classic. Humor me and make your old dad happy. I want only the best for my beautiful girls. You and your mother always were my greatest joy.*

"*Signed, Your loving, concerned father, Matthew Duchess, February 2, Kingston, New York.*"

When Mr. Carlson finished reading the letter and looked up, Greer turned her blond head to eye her fair-haired sisters seated around the table.

Because their dad's health had been deteriorating long before they'd buried him six weeks ago, they'd already been through the most painful part of their mourning period. Certainly with all the bills owing to the extra health care costs for both their mom and dad, the idea of an inheritance had never crossed their minds.

To find out their parents had left them any money at all came as a total surprise. But the mention of a Husband Fund completely soured the gift for Greer.

Not only that…she balked at the idea of being forced to view the film their funny, dear mom must have seen too many times to count.

It was one of those Hollywood movies about three women who decide to get married and scheme to find a millionaire in the process. However their mother had never been able to get Greer to watch it because Greer found the concept utterly absurd.

If a woman wanted that kind of money, she didn't need a man. All she had to do was become a millionaire herself!

But their mother had been born in a different era with a completely different mind-set about a woman's choices in life.

Being a hopeless romantic, she'd named her nonidentical triplets for her favorite movie stars. In fact she'd raised her daughters on fairy tales.

Greer had never been a great proponent of them.

While Olivia and Piper swooned over the beautiful girl ending up with the handsome prince just because she was beautiful, Greer often upset her sisters by fabricating her own renditions.

She much preferred that the beautiful, innocent, helpless heroine use her brain to figure out a financial scheme to buy the castle and lands from Prince Charming who needed a lot more going for him than charm to attract her and win her hand in marriage.

Greer had shocked their mother when she'd told her it was probably a man who'd thought up all those fractured fairy tales.

It wasn't that Greer had anything against men per se. In fact she loved to date and often tripled dated with her sisters. Don and his friends had been the latest bunch of guys they'd gone out with as a group. But she drew the line at a serious relationship.

There was plenty of time for marriage in the future. Her own parents hadn't married until much later in life when they were finally ready to settle down and have a family. That was good enough for her.

Many times Greer, the oldest of the triplets who'd always espoused the "all for one, one for all" theory, had told her sisters that getting married would spoil the fun of building the business they'd started from scratch to see how far they could take it.

She glanced back at the attorney. "Do we have to stay and watch the film?"

"Only if you want your five thousand dollars. That was your father's stipulation. If you choose not to sit through the viewing, I'm to give the money to the cancer foundation in your mother's memory." His brows lifted. "For what it's worth, I've seen it several times and enjoy it more every time."

Greer rolled her eyes in disbelief, ready to bolt, but her sisters made no move to leave. Deep down she knew why. As much as the three of them hated the idea of being a captive audience to such a ridiculous movie, they were faced with a moral dilemma.

Because of the restrictions about the money, it was no good to them and would never be spent. But they couldn't walk out now. That would be like throwing everything back in their parents' faces. The sobering realization that they'd had the best mother and father in the world kept them nailed to their chairs.

After crossing one long, elegant leg over the other, Greer waited while Mr. Carlson, who had to be in his seventies, moved the TV closer.

Once he started the DVD, she sat back in the leather chair prepared to suffer through another story no doubt written, produced and cast by men, for men.

Not only was the movie much worse than she'd thought, Mr. Carlson was glued to the screen, glassy eyed. Ten minutes into the film and Greer had to bite her lip to keep from bursting into laughter.

Flashing her sisters a covert glance, she sensed they were having the same problem. But out of respect for their father's wishes, they managed to contain themselves.

When the show came to an end, a collective silence filled the room before Mr. Carlson realized it was time to shut off the DVD.

He turned to them. "Would thirty days give you girls enough time to vacate the house?"

"We've already moved to Mrs. Weyland's basement apartment across the street from us," Greer informed him.

The girls nodded. "We left our home spotless."

"The keys are in this envelope along with a paper that lists our cell phone numbers and the address of our new apartment." Greer pushed it toward him before she shot out of her chair, ready to go.

He rose more slowly and handed them their checks. "You're as remarkable and self-sufficient as your father always told me you were. Yet I could hope for your sakes you'll take your parents' advice." He stared pointedly at Greer. "Women weren't meant to be on their own."

The man's sincerity couldn't be doubted. But his comment happened to be one of the twelve comments appearing on the calendar she'd thought up last year featuring Men's Most Notable Quotes About Women. The calendar had been an instant success.

Greer didn't dare look at her sisters or she would have cracked up on the spot. Hilarity had been building inside her. She couldn't stifle it any longer. They had to get out of there quick!

"Thank you for everything, Mr. Carlson."

So saying, Greer made a beeline for the door, clutching the check in hand. Her sisters followed.

They hurried down the hall to the crowded elevator. By some miracle they reached their father's old Pontiac parked around the corner before they exploded with laughter.

Since Olivia had a better sense of direction than the others, she always drove them when they were together.

"After the first close-up of Betty Grable, I thought we were going to have to call emergency for Mr. Carlson!"

"That generation's hopeless."

"The movie was dreadful!"

"But our mother loved it, bless her heart."

"And Daddy loved her!"

"And we loved both of them, so what are we going to do about the—"

"No—" Greer blurted. "Don't say the 'H' word."

For the rest of the drive home they giggled like schoolgirls instead of twenty-seven-year-old women.

When they pulled to a stop at the curb across the street from their old house, Olivia looked over her shoulder at Greer who was seated in the back. "Let's go get us a new car. This one already has 122,000 miles on it."

That sounded like her impulsive sister. "Right this minute?"

"Why not?"

Before Greer could negate the suggestion, Piper, the romantic, shook her head. "With fifteen thousand dollars to put down, we could buy a new house. What do you think?"

Greer, the pragmatic one, said, "I think I'm too exhausted to think." It came out sounding grumpy because the Husband Fund money was untouchable and they all knew it.

"Mrs. Weyland says we need a vacation," Olivia muttered.

Piper rested her head against the window. "I'd love to visit the Caribbean."

"Who wouldn't, but we can't go."

Both sisters blinked. "Why not?"

Greer leaned forward. "Because it's April. By the time we could get away from the business, it would be June. I think we could run into a hurricane."

"How do you know that?"

"Our northeast distributor, Jan. She scuba dives there in February when the weather is perfect."

"Then how about Hawaii?"

Olivia wrinkled her nose at Piper. "Everybody complains it's too touristy. I'd rather go someplace more exotic, like Tahiti."

"The airfare alone would be exorbitant."

"So what's your suggestion?" Both sisters were waiting for Greer's answer.

"I don't have one, and you guys know why."

Olivia's eyes resembled the blue in a match flame when she felt strongly about something. "Then we'll go through the motions of husband hunting in some wonderful place like Australia where the beaches are reputed to be the most beautiful in the world. Mrs. Weyland's right, you know? We haven't had a break in several years."

By now Piper's irises were glowing an iridescent blue-green. "Daddy didn't say we had to *end up* with a husband."

Greer could acknowledge she had a point. "You're right. All he said was, you can spend the money any way you want so long as it's used in the *pursuit* of a spouse. With $5,000 apiece, we should be able to go someplace exciting for a couple of weeks. I'm all for visiting the Great Barrier Reef."

"Or South America!" Olivia interjected. "Don't forget Rio. Ipanema and Copacabana are supposed to be two of the most fabulous beaches on earth."

"Wait a minute—" Piper spread her hands in front of her. "Wherever we decide to spend our vacation, I've got this delicious idea how we'll provide the bait to bring the men on fast!"

Olivia smiled. "I bet I know what you're thinking."

So did Greer. They'd all watched that idiotic film and

weren't triplets for nothing. "You mean turn things around by pretending *we're* the millionaires?"

"Why not?"

Why not indeed. Greer realized it was a stretch, but if her business projections held true, they'd be doing very well for themselves by the time they were thirty.

"Guys—" Piper broke in with dramatic flourish. "We have a lot more going for us than money. We're *titled!* Ladies and gentlemen, may I present the Duchesses of Kingston!"

*Brilliant.*

So brilliant in fact, Greer was still staring at her talented sister in wonder when Olivia suddenly blurted, *"The Duchesse pendant!"*

No one's mind could leap faster from A to Z than Olivia's.

"Yes?" Greer prompted. "What about it?"

The pendant was a gold rectangle. It was encrusted with amethysts surrounding a pearl-studded pigeon with a red-orange eye of pyrope garnet.

According to the story their dad told them, a court artisan fashioned the pendant for the Duchess of Parma, otherwise known as Marie-Louise of Austria of the House of Bourbon. On the back of the pendant was a stylized "D" and "P."

When she died, one of her children inherited it, and then it was given to a granddaughter who passed it down through the Duchesse line until it fell into their father's hands.

In anticipation of their sixteenth birthday, Greer's parents had gone to a jeweler who'd had two matching pendants fashioned using the original for a model so each of their daughters could have the same memento.

"For your children to cherish," their parents had said, giving them a loving hug and kiss along with the gift.

Eleven years later and their daughters were still single. Greer assumed that one day they'd all be married and have families. She just didn't know when, and couldn't have cared less.

"Think, my dear duchesses!" Olivia grinned. "Where is there a lovely beach with a whole bunch of gorgeous playboys running around looking to marry a titled woman wearing the family jewels?"

"*The Riviera,* of course."

"Of course!" Greer's sisters cried.

"Except that we came through the illegitimate line of the House of Parma-Bourbon," she reminded them.

"Who cares? We *are* related!"

"Only if the story's true."

"Daddy seemed to think it was," Piper reasoned, "otherwise how would he have ended up with the pendant?"

"Somebody could have made up a tall tale about it that grew legs down through the years," Greer reminded her sisters. "Still, we *do* have it in our possession, and no one's been able to prove we're not related. Anyway, you've given me an idea.

"We know Marie-Louise went by three other titles; Duchess of Colorno, Duchess of Piacenza and Duchess of Guastalla. So what if we each took a title representing our relationship to her? We could outcon all the playboys we want."

At this point her sisters stared in awe at Greer whose eyes reflected the exact color of the Duchess of Parma violet.

The flower had been named for their ancestor who loved violets so much, when she wrote letters she often left the imprint of the flower rather than her signature.

A conspiratorial smile broke out on Olivia's face. "I say we start on the Italian Riviera with one side trip to Parma and Colorno to see the palaces where she lived.

Then work our way along the coast to the French and Spanish Riviera, letting it be known we've been in Italy visiting our…royal relations?''

Brilliant! Sometimes Olivia's innovative ideas reflected pure genius.

Greer's thoughts leaped ahead. ''We'll do business while we're there so we can write off our trip as an expense on our taxes. It shouldn't be difficult to find someone to translate our calendars into various languages and distribute them for us. It might be the start of something really big.''

Piper's eyes gleamed. ''In time Violetta and Luigio could become household words all over Europe. Just don't forget we'll have to honor Daddy's wishes by trying our hardest to snag a husband at the same time,'' she reminded them.

''It'll be a piece of cake,'' Olivia declared. ''As soon as we let it be known we're duchesses, our unsuspecting victims will fall all over us.''

''And we know why, don't we,'' Greer said with a definite smirk. ''Because they're nothing but a bunch of impoverished adventurers who prey on wealthy women and prefer to marry a titled one if possible.'' One delicately arched brow lifted.

''Their black moment will come when we smile sweetly and admit we're the *poor* American duchesses. 'Sorry. No tiara.' So if they want to take back their proposals…''

Piper shook her head at Greer. ''You're wicked.''

''Terrible,'' Olivia concurred.

''Not as terrible as *they* are. Just watch the bodies fall!'' Greer eyed her sisters with unholy glee. ''Let's go inside and make our plans while we eat lunch.''

Piper was the first one out of the car. Olivia followed. ''If we hurry, we can apply for passports before the place closes today.''

Greer brought up the rear. "Airfares are really cheap to Europe right now, which is good news since we'll need new wardrobes."

"If we're going to do this thing right, maybe we should charter a private yacht."

"I'm way ahead of you but I don't think we could afford it."

"It wouldn't hurt to find out," Olivia said. "Maybe if it were a small one?"

Once inside the apartment Greer hurried over to the computer in the living room, which they'd made into their office. The girls hovered around while she did a dozen searches of yachting services.

"Hmm. I'm afraid they're out of our price range. So far the best we can do is charter a crewed sailboat for twelve people. It's $5,000 a week per person if the boat is full at the time of departure. That's no good."

Piper leaned over Greer's shoulder. "Just for fun, click to the crewed catamaran listings. It's says they're cheaper."

When the information appeared on the screen, they studied the names of the boats with avid interest.

"Look!" Olivia blurted. "There's one called the *Piccione*."

Greer had already spotted the Italian word for pigeon. Their dad had always called his daughters his "pigeons" because of the beautiful white Duchesse pigeon the Italians had named in honor of the Duchess of Parma. Just for fun she clicked to it. After the specifics popped up, she read them aloud.

"This immaculate, white, fifty-one-foot sloop sleeps two to six guests. Crew of three. Full amenities, three meals per day. $3,000 per person. Ten days on the Mediterranean.

"*Ten* guys! Plan your own itinerary. The swift way to

get close to any beach. Contact F. Moretti, Vernazza, Italy.''

Olivia nudged Greer. ''That's what you call exclusive at the right price. It must be destiny! E-mail them and find out if they have any openings left for this summer or early fall.''

''Do we care which month?''

They both shook their heads.

After sending an inquiry, Greer joined them in the kitchen. They hurriedly ate sandwiches before rummaging around for their birth certificates.

Once those were found, they left for the passport office. En route they stopped to get their passport pictures taken, reminding them they all needed a new hairdo to go with their new duchess look.

An hour later they started for home. On the way Piper noticed a travel agency. She told Olivia to stop the car so she could run inside and get some brochures.

On the way back to the apartment, they almost got into an argument because everyone wanted to savor the brochure on Vernazza. Greer had to admit the place sounded like heaven.

*One of the most unspoilt areas of the Mediterranean. To visit Vernazza is to visit the Cinque Terre, a kingdom of nature and wild scents; five villages suspended between sea and sky, clinging on to cliffs and surrounded by green hills. Who visits Cinque Terre can choose between a dive in the sea, a hike in the hills, a walk in the narrow ''carruggi,'' or a boat trip to a sanctuary or to a seafood lunch.*

Piper was the first to reach the computer after they'd entered the apartment.

''We've got an answer to our e-mail!''

Greer and Olivia leaned over her shoulder while she read it to them.

''Thank you for your inquiry. Due to an unexpected

cancellation, the June 18 slot is available. *Woohoo!*'' She jumped up and down in the swivel chair.

''You are very fortunate since the twentieth is the date of the Grand Prix in Monaco where we have docking privileges. If you wish to take advantage, you must advise us immediately.''

Piper swung around in the chair. ''Monaco, guys. The playground of the rich and 'wannabe' rich and famous. The Grand Prix! Think, Olivia— Maybe you'll be able to see that dashing French race car driver you talk about all the time. The one that puts Fred's nose out of joint every time you mention him.''

''It's Fred's fault if he introduced me to Formula I racing. Wouldn't it be something to bring home Cesar Villon's autograph?'' Olivia's eyes were shining.

Greer was thinking it would be even more exciting to meet an Italian from their own Duchesse family who could provide the documentation proving their relationship to the Duchess of Parma.

''Piper? Find out if they'll accept another thousand a piece from us so we can have the boat to ourselves.''

''Ooh, I forgot about that, Greer. Good idea. I don't dare tell Tom about this or he'll want to come along.''

''What he doesn't know won't hurt him. It isn't as if you're in love with him.''

''How do you know?''

''Well are you?''

''Maybe.''

''Then ten days away from him will prove it one way or the other. Right?''

''I suppose so.'' Piper finished typing the question and sent an instant message.

While they waited for an answer, Greer studied one of the brochures with a map detailing the Mediterranean coastline bordering Europe.

Another shriek of delight came out of Piper. "They're willing if we pay in full now."

"Before we commit, we've got to find out if we can get plane reservations," Greer cautioned.

"I've already inquired." Olivia put her hand over the mouthpiece. "Everything's booked solid into Milan, Rome and Bologna, but we could still get seats to Genoa for June 16, returning June 29."

Greer looked at the map once more. "That's only fifty or so miles from Vernazza," she estimated aloud. "We could take a train and find a hotel for the 17 and 28. Book those flights for us, Olivia!"

Piper turned to Greer. "How do we want to pay for the boat?"

She pulled the wallet out of her purse. "Here. Use our business credit card to pay the bill in full. Let them know it's the Duchess of Kingston of the House of Parma-Bourbon making a reservation for an exclusive party of three, and you want that information kept confidential."

When the deed was done, their laughter bounced off the living-room walls.

"That was good thinking, Greer. Now it's guaranteed word will leak out," Olivia murmured. "We'll have to arrive at the dock looking sensational."

"Oh—" Piper cried. "You just made me think of something else. Remember that Paris elevator scene in the film about the American girl whose fiancé falls in love with a French girl? Remember the knockout dress she had on?"

Olivia's delicate brows arched. "Who could forget? We ought to be able to find inexpensive outfits and beachwear like the ones she wore. Maybe a hat or two? No one will know we didn't pay a fortune for them."

"Not if we wear our pendants," Piper inserted.

"Exactly. The men we're targeting survive by going after women with jewels. Without a jeweler's loupe, they won't be able to detect the fakes from the original." To this day Greer couldn't tell the difference.

"Then it's settled! We'll arrive in Italy wearing our pendants and see what happens! Since we have to stay at a hotel the first night we get there, I say we make a big splash. What's the most exclusive one in Genoa?"

"Just a sec, Olivia."

Piper got busy on the Internet once more. "Hmm...how about the Splendido in nearby Portofino, first discovered by the Duke of Windsor. 'Preferred by royals overlooking Portofino harbor, gateway to the Riviera.' Twelve hundred Eurodollars a night for the three of us. It's about twenty-five miles from the airport and they have limo service. Do you guys think it's worth it?"

Both Greer and Olivia nodded.

"So do I. Let me check to see if there's a room available for the seventeenth. By the time the twenty-eighth rolls around, we'll have had our fun and can stay in a youth hostel if our funds are running low."

Greer's eyes narrowed. "A hostel will be the perfect place to invite our 'would be' husbands when we drop our little bombs."

Olivia started chuckling. "You have no heart."

"You're scary," Piper told Greer.

She gave them her innocent look. "Did Cinderella have a choice when the carriage turned into a pumpkin on the way home, leaving her with one glass slipper?

"Can *we* help it if all we'll have to show for our attendance at the ball is the pendant we were wearing when we arrived?"

# CHAPTER TWO

*June 17, House of Lords, England*

"MY LORDS, we will begin by hearing the opening statement from Signore Maximilliano di Varano of the House of Parma-Bourbon. He is the chief counselor avvocato for the Emilia-Romagna Farmers Consorzio of Italy, of which the Federazione del Prosciutto de Parma, a member, is the appellant in the case brought against the United Kingdom Supermarket Cartel, known as UKSC, represented by Lord Winthrope."

Back in the House of Lords for the second time in a year, Max got to his feet, determined his appeal would force the case to be moved to the European Court of Justice for a definitive decision.

"Thank you, my lords," he began with virtually no trace of accent, thanks to an elite private school education that included four years at Oxford and extensive travel in the U.S. and Canada with his cousins.

"To refresh your memories, Prosciutto de Parma, or Parma ham, has been made in Parma from pigs reared in northern and central Italy since Etruscan times. It is famous throughout the world with a name that is a protected designation of origin.

"The Corona Ducale, a five-pointed coronet symbolizing the ancient Duchy of Parma, is the outward guarantee of authenticity. According to Italian law, it has to appear upon the product in whatever form it is sold to the customer. If he buys a complete ham, or slices cut up at a shop, it has to bear the brand. If he buys prepackaged slices, it must appear stamped on the package.

"The second respondent, Prime Choice Affiliates, is a reputable food processor in Herefordshire that prepares packages of authentic Parma ham slices and pieces to be sold to the first respondent, UKSC, which sells them to the public in its supermarkets. Unfortunately it's done *without* the Corona Ducale on the package.

"The Federazione del Prosciutto de Parma maintains this is an unlawful practice under Italian law, as well as European law, enforceable in the courts of all the member states.

"In the present proceedings, the Federazione claims a continuing injunction against Prime Choice Affiliates and the UKSC, restraining them from marketing the packages as Parma ham until the European Court of Justice can hear the case and make a definitive ruling. I now yield my time back to Lord Winthrope."

When Max sat down, his assistant, Bernaldo, handed him a note.

With one ear taking in the QC's opening remarks, he read the message. But his mind was focused on the case to the degree that it didn't register until he'd read it a second time.

*Your secretary in Colorno just received a call from the head of security at Cristoforo Colombo airport in Genoa Sestri. You're to phone Fausto Galli at 555 328 as soon as possible. It's a classified matter of great importance.*

Translated, it meant there was no crisis such as his own personal family or extended family being injured in an accident or some such thing. Relieved, he put the message in his suit pocket, making a mental note to call Signore Galli back during the recess.

For ten minutes Max listened while the QC pontificated. Finally the man came to the point.

"In my view there exists a fair argument that the supervisory role of the Parma Federation in ensuring that only the genuine product is sold as Parma ham, has been discharged once it leaves the Parma area. I yield back to Signore di Varano."

Once again Max got up from the chair. "My lords, the issue here is whether the Federazione del Prosciutto de Parma's prohibitions contained in a legislative measure of a member state can achieve community wide effect to the U.K. and elsewhere. Therefore I respectfully appeal this case to the European Court of Justice. Otherwise it will continue to remain at an impasse which achieves nothing for either party."

Following his remarks, presiding judge Lord Marbury announced a fifteen-minute recess. Curious to discover what the call from Genoa was all about, Max pulled the cell phone from his breast pocket and dialed the number written on the paper.

He only had to wait two rings before he heard a male voice say, "*Pronto*. Signore di Varano?"

"*Si?*"

"It is an honor to speak to you. I have some news that I know will be of great interest to your family. Since you handle its legal affairs, I felt it prudent to alert you first."

"Go ahead, signore."

"A half hour ago three American women passed through customs after deboarding their flight from New York. My men detained them using the excuse they were vetting incoming passengers for information due to a suspicious person being aboard the plane. In truth, it was discovered they're each wearing the Duchesse pendant."

"Each?" Max shook his dark head in exasperation. "That's impossible!"

There was only *one* pendant in existence, but it could be anywhere because well over a year ago the Duchess of

Parma jewelry collection on display at the family palace in Colorno had been stolen.

The pendant was the least valuable of the items taken in terms of monetary worth, however its historical and sentimental value was inestimable, especially to Max's family.

"Did you consult an expert?"

"*Si.* During the interrogation, photographs were taken. They were enhanced for our forensics expert who compared them against the photo of the pendant you had distributed to the police after the theft. They were a perfect match."

Max blinked in astonishment.

"That's why I'm calling you, Signore di Varano. Do you wish me to confiscate the pendants so they can be examined? So far the Americans still don't know why they're being detained."

"That's good. Let's leave it that way for now. I appreciate your discretion and quick thinking, Signore Galli. You've handled the situation perfectly.

"However we've had many leads since news of the theft was made public and a reward for its return was offered. So far all the leads have turned out to be false. But I must admit this little joke initiated by some brazen Americans was meant to draw attention for a reason. One can only wonder why."

"My very thought, particularly since the joke gets even stranger."

The odd inflection in the other man's voice intrigued Max. "Explain what you mean."

"They're sisters."

"You mean professed nuns?"

"No, no. They are the same age with the same birthday."

"Triplets?" You didn't see that every day. "How old are they?"

*"Ventisette."*

Twenty-seven and already leading a life of crime…

*"Molto bellissima!"*

Beautiful, of course.

"Their paperwork states they are the Duchesses of Kingston from New York."

Duchesses of Kingston?

Max flicked his gaze to Lord Winthrope. *If* such a title existed, the esteemed QC would know who they were in an instant.

"Unfortunately I'm in London and can't return to Genoa before evening to investigate this matter. Did you find out their purpose for being in Italy?"

"They claim to be on vacation with a little business thrown in. We checked the information they gave us. It's been verified they're booked at the Splendido tonight and have chartered a sailboat for tomorrow."

"From Portofino?"

"No. Vernazza."

A frown slowly replaced Max's smile. That little bombshell hit too close to home to be a coincidence.

Two years ago he'd given the *Piccione* to his good friend Fabio and his two younger brothers after their parents had been lost at sea in the family fishing boat. The Morettis now made their living crewing for tourists.

To his friend's credit and business prowess, he'd paid Max back every last Euro, though Max had never asked or expected repayment. For twenty months like clockwork he'd received a good-size installment with a note of heartfelt gratitude from the man he didn't see nearly as often as he would have liked.

Besides watching after his brothers, Fabio now had a wife and they were expecting their second baby. Since they ran the only sailboat charter business in the tiny town which had been Max's backyard growing up, he knew exactly where to find these Americans. That is *if* they intended to stick to their agenda once they were freed to leave the airport.

"You may release them, Signore Galli, but have them followed and closely watched. After my flight touches down I'll make contact with you."

*"Bene. Arrivederci."*

After hanging up the phone, Max wrote a note on his scratch pad. He asked Bernaldo to hand carry it to Lord Winthrope. "Wait for his answer and bring it back to me."

Bernaldo went off to do Max's bidding. He returned a few minutes later. Max opened the note, eager to read what the other man had to say in response.

Glad to be of help, Max.

Evelyn Pierrepont succeeded his grandfather as the second duke of Kingston. He was primarily famous for his liaison with Elizabeth Chudleigh, who claimed to be the Duchess of Kingston, but the Kingston titles became extinct on the duke's death around 1733. He had no children. Hope that answers your question.

Indeed it did.

Max lifted his head and smiled at Lord Winthrope who smiled back.

So…these American women weren't only audacious imposters, their impudence showed a certain shrewdness to pick an English title that had become extinct over two hundred years ago and pass it off as their own.

What kind of a game were they playing to come to Italy wearing pendants identical to the stolen one? Where did they get such an idea? Why would they do it?

"Much as I'd love to run to the room and change into my swimming suit, I'm too tired."

"Jet lag's caught up with me, too. Let's go to bed. You coming, Greer?"

"In a minute—"

The magic of the balmy Genoese night held her in its thrall. She'd always dreamed of coming to Italy. Though ninety percent of their ancestry was English and Scotch-Irish, their father had favored their Italian-Austrian roots. As a result he'd infected Greer with that love.

"Okay. Just don't make noise when you let yourself in."

"I promise," she said before their footsteps faded.

After several business meetings which might or might not produce a foothold in Europe, followed by a late dinner, they'd taken a walk to the San Giorgio church and visited the interior.

From there they'd strolled around the tropical gardens on the grounds of the Splendido, a former sixteenth-century monastery. They'd finally ended up at its outdoor pool overlooking Portofino harbor.

In Greer's opinion the view was worth a king's ransom. How their mother would have loved this flower-scented paradise.

There were quite a few guests climbing in and out of the water. Waiters moved around unobtrusively refilling champagne glasses. Every so often Greer caught snatches of conversation and laughter from beautiful men and women enjoying the elegant amenities of the privileged class.

As she stood next to a palm tree wearing her designer sundress in a stunning tangerine color, her attention was caught by a man doing laps with the speed and fluidity of a shark. A great black shark, if there were such a thing she mused fancifully.

Glimpses of a bronzed, well-toned male physique and

jet-black hair kept her gaze riveted. Suddenly he levered himself from the water onto the tiled deck.

The shark had legs.

Strong, powerful legs that propelled his tall, black trunk-clad body past the admiring glances from women and the envious stares of men toward Greer.

His total disregard of the surroundings testified to his inbuilt radar system which had targeted its next victim. How easy her subconscious had made it for him by sending out the message that she wanted to see if all of him lived up to her image of the quintessential playboy.

All of him did...

From an aquiline face, whose Italian bones had been refined and molded down through the centuries, gleamed a pair of black eyes that resembled volcanoes erupting in the night sky. One intimate look from them beneath expressive black brows and she felt as if her body had come too close to the mesmerizing magma.

Burned alive would be the more accurate description.

The pulse in her throat throbbed so violently, she could feel it move the pendant she wore around her neck like a choker.

She watched him watching it. He'd taken the bait.

Piper would be especially pleased to find out her suggestion to wear the family heirloom had proved to be a winner their first night in Italy.

"I saw you walking on the grounds earlier, *signorina*." His heavily accented English delivered in a deep masculine voice, vibrated to her insides. Its cadence sent a delicious tremor through her system even though the night was warm. "I hoped you would come to the pool."

Of course he did.

"I noticed you, too," she responded boldly, for once throwing her innate caution to the wind. "That's why I didn't go upstairs with my sisters."

It was a lie. She hadn't seen him. He was too much of a predator to have given himself away beforehand. Like his species, he'd lurked in the depths until it was time to make his attack.

"Swim with me."

His ardent demand, whispered with a pulsating urgency that said his life wouldn't be worth living if she didn't consent, decided her.

"I'm not wearing a suit."

"Does it matter?" came the breathtaking question.

She could have toyed with him a trifle longer and enjoyed every provocative minute of it. But in the end she decided not to tempt fate.

"No."

The second she said the word, she saw something flare in the dark recesses of his eyes.

Had she surprised him with her answer? To her knowledge sharks didn't have human emotions, only instincts that led them to their nearest prey.

*Well, here I am... Let's see how long it takes you to swallow me.*

With great daring she slipped off her gold sandals, left her gold watch and gold lame clutch bag on a table near the deep end of the pool, then dove in headfirst.

Having lived along the Hudson River all their lives, their father had taught Greer and her sisters to be strong swimmers. As a result, it was their favorite sport which they enjoyed on a regular basis.

The bottom of this pool was tiled in a fabulous design. She swam lower to get a better look, but was halted in her quest when a strong pair of male hands found her hips and brought her swiftly to the surface.

She emerged with her neck-length hair plastered around her head, no longer the picture of classic royal grace. Unfortunately that wasn't what disturbed her. It was the fact that her dress had ridden up to her waist, which meant nothing was separating his hands from her skin except her underwear.

With his arresting face only centimeters from hers, she would have to put on the performance of her life not to let him know how alarmed she was by this shocking turn of events.

"We haven't been properly introduced. My name is Greer Duchess."

"Greer," he repeated softly. The way he pronounced it made even the hard "G" sound beautiful. His slow white smile dazzled her. "Your name is as unique as you are. What brings a beautiful American woman like you to Italy?"

It was time to try out the story she'd rehearsed. "My sisters and I are here to visit relatives."

"Ah, yes?"

"Yes. My ancestor was the Duchess of Colorno."

His black eyes flared in recognition. "You're referring to Maria-Luigia of Austria of the House of Parma-Bourbon?"

So he knew his Italian history well enough to recognize the Duchesse pendant! This was so easy it was scary!

She couldn't wait to tell Olivia and Piper she'd caught a real playboy on her first night! Now all she had to do was play him for a while before she reeled him in and got him to propose marriage.

When she unmasked herself, he would slip off the hook and swim away. Then she would be able to enjoy the rest of this fabulous vacation knowing she'd followed her father's stipulation about the Husband Fund to the letter.

"Yes. That's right. My sisters and I are the American descendants from her Duchesse line." No need to add "the illegitimate line" at this juncture. "Now that I've told you something about myself, I'd like to know who *you* are,'' she said in the most seductive tone she could produce.

''Why don't you guess my name?'' he came back in a deep voice that was equally tantalizing.

As if to emphasize his remark, she felt his thumbs making lazy circles against the nylon, increasing her awareness of him while they tread water. Her insides turned to liquid.

She gazed at his incredible male beauty through veiled eyes and said the first thing that popped into her head. ''Luigio?''

His lips twitched, as if what she'd said had truly amused him. ''No.''

Greer had never been this daring in her life. But something about the man was like an elixir in her veins, increasing her bravado. She flashed him a brilliant smile. ''This might take a long time.''

He gave an elegant shrug of his broad Italian shoulders before drawing her closer. ''I've been in London on business. Now I'm on vacation for the next week and would love nothing better than to spend every second of it with you, *bellissima.*''

Every second? That meant day *and* night. She just bet he would!

To her consternation she realized she would love the same thing. A shiver of delight ran through her body.

She'd always heard the expression ''carnal thoughts,'' but she'd never understood their true meaning until now...

Greer could find no fault in this Italian heartthrob who had it all down pat. Most likely he'd just left a woman in London and was now on the lookout for his next conquest.

As long as she was the bait with jewels and a title, why not tease him for a while longer first. She had an idea it would be a new experience for him.

''Unfortunately my sisters and I are leaving for Vernazza in the morning and won't be back.''

"I know it well. Since you show no fear of the water, I would be happy to take you to a secret grotto which can only be reached by swimming a short distance beneath the sea."

She flashed him an artless smile. "Like Edmond Dantes who found Abbe Faria's treasure on Monte Cristo, will I discover gold and silver and precious pearls?"

His hard-muscled body stilled before he cocked his dark, handsome head. Even wet, his vibrant hair had a tendency to curl. "Is that what you're looking for?"

Again she had the oddest sensation that she'd said something unexpected, something that puzzled him. "Isn't everyone searching for treasure that will bring them ultimate happiness?"

"Ultimate happiness?" he murmured the words as if to himself, but his gaze was playing over her features, dwelling on each feminine attribute for heart-stopping seconds. "What is that I wonder?"

The philosopher emerging from the adventurer. He was a better actor than she'd first supposed.

"Thanks to Alexandre Dumas, we do know one thing…"

"That's right," he whispered. His lips were so close she could feel the warmth of his breath on hers. In reaction her toes curled against his hair-roughened legs as their limbs tangled beneath the water. "Though the Count of Monte Cristo had his revenge against his enemies, he didn't find happiness after all."

"Except that Dumas's book was a tale of fiction," she countered.

Again his eyes glimmered like black fires burning on a distant hill. "If you wish, I will take you to the island of Monte Cristo. It's not far from Vernazza. Perhaps there you will find what you're looking for."

You mean *you*, of course.

She struggled not to laugh at the pure conceit of the man. "Perhaps."

"Does that mean—"

"It means...perhaps," she interrupted with a flirtatious smile. "Now I'm tired and must say good night."

His hands remained fastened on her hips. "But it's not late, and you're too young to be tired."

"True, but we just flew in today, and were detained by the police while we were going through customs. Three hours to be exact. It was very exhausting."

"I'm sorry such a terrible thing happened to you in my country. Why would the police do this?"

"The head of security said there was a suspicious person on board our jet. He and his men took statements from the passengers who sat near this person."

"Were you able to help?"

"I don't know. We tried to remember the people seated around us, but no one looked suspicious to me. When we were finally let go, all we wanted was to reach our hotel and go to sleep."

"Of course," he whispered with compassion. His eyes wandered over her in intense appraisal before he said, *"Momento—"*

With one hand still possessively molding the curve of her hip, he signaled a waiter, rapping out something in rapid Italian. The other man nodded and disappeared.

Reading the question in her eyes, her captor explained, "I asked him to bring you a robe to wear back to your room. Such a delectable sight should not be for everyone's eyes."

Only *yours,* and you've been drinking your fill with unabashed enjoyment, she thought. He played it just right. The lothario with a streak of chivalry to keep him from being a complete cad.

"Thank you, Signore…Mysterioso," she improvised in her best Italian which, sadly, left a lot to be desired.

A bark of laughter escaped his throat, the first unorchestrated response to come out of him. In that millisecond of time she was allowed a glimpse of what lay beneath the polished veneer and felt an emotional tug totally foreign to her.

Not wishing to delve any deeper into her suddenly confused emotions, she arched backward to escape his grasp and struck out for the shallow end. That way she could use the steps and retain some semblance of dignity.

However he managed to get there first. In a surprisingly protective gesture, he placed the extended white toweling robe around her shoulders. She was quite amazed at the speed with which the waiter had obeyed the stranger's command without question.

She raised violet eyes to meet the smoldering depths of his. "Thank you. I was feeling a little vulnerable."

"Like Venus rising from the sea?" he suggested.

The second the words came out of his mouth, Greer could picture the famous painting of the Roman goddess of beauty awakening from a seashell without any clothes on.

Greer blushed at the shocking analogy and turned her head away. But he made the situation even more explosive and intimate by lifting the pendant and lowering his head to kiss the tiny pulse fluttering madly beneath it.

"One day soon when we have no audience except the sun on our skin and the sand beneath our bodies, I hope to see you exactly as Botticelli created her," he murmured against her scented throat.

Between the sensuality of his remark and the brush of his lips branding her heated flesh, she drew in an audible breath before wheeling away from his grasp.

Trembling, she plucked her watch and purse from the

table where she'd left them. Before she could decide whether to wear or carry her high heels, he'd looped his index finger through the gold straps.

"I'll escort you to your room. Not even the Splendido can guarantee the safety of a woman on her own who looks like you. In your exhausted state you would be no match for someone who would like to spirit you away to some secret lagoon for the night…"

The image he'd created sent another shiver through her body, part ecstasy, part fright.

Before this trip, the playboys Greer had pictured in her mind were likable. Manageable. Easy come, easy go.

Maybe a little miffed to recognize they'd been conned, but gallant enough to salute the girls as worthy adversaries who'd pulled off a well-executed charade. No hard feelings as they made their charming retreat from the playing field.

Up until this moment she'd been enjoying a game that had its nascence back in Kingston two months earlier. But just now when he'd kissed her and whispered his daring remark, she'd sensed a power shift.

Now *he* was the one dangling her as surely as he dangled her shoes from his fingers.

Instinct told her this was a dangerous man, the kind you didn't lure back to a youth hostel to tell him "sorry, wrong duchess." *He* would be the one to decide when he was tired of playing, then he would move in for the kill. Until then he would keep her trapped in his sights, and there'd be no place for her to hide.

A thrill of alarm caused her to walk faster.

When they reached the elevator where other guests were coming and going, she was in a state of panic and used the brief interim to extricate the hotel room key from her purse.

However by the time they'd exited onto the third floor, reason had reasserted itself. She told herself it was lack of

sleep that had made her so uneasy. She would be leaving
the hotel tomorrow and since she had no intention of ever
seeing him again, she was even able to smile up at him
with renewed confidence.

After the long transatlantic flight followed by a grueling
three hours detainment at the hands of the police, she
hadn't been herself at all. Otherwise she wouldn't have
given a perfect stranger the green light to pursue her.

For a woman to plunge into the pool with her clothes
on in order to sink her hooks into him, what else was a
man like him supposed to think?

Tonight had been an experiment. A dry run. Whoops.
A wet one, she mused nervously to herself, realizing her
emotions bordered on hysteria.

She'd blown it, but she'd learned from it. Tomorrow
would be a new day filled with more playboys and fresh
possibilities.

The hotel room door was in sight. With one fluid movement she unlocked it, but before she could slip inside, he
left a kiss on the side of her neck that set her whole body
on fire. "Until tomorrow."

His promise sounded more like an avowal.

"Goodbye," she announced through the crack in the
door before shutting it hard and locking it.

Congratulating herself on making it safely to her room,
she staggered over to the nearest chair and held on while
she attempted to recover from her fright. Her clutch bag
fell to the floor with a soft thud.

Too late she remembered he still had her shoes. No matter. She didn't need them. In truth, she never wanted to
see them again. She never wanted to see *him* again.

# CHAPTER THREE

THE lights went on.

"Greer?" The second her sisters saw the condition she was in, they scrambled out of their beds toward her.

"How come your dress is wet?"

"Where did you get that robe?

"Where are your shoes?"

The questions pelting her one after the other stripped her down to the bare bones. This was no laughing matter. The only reason she'd escaped at all was that *he'd* allowed it.

She could still see the mixture of triumph and mockery glinting from the black depths of his eyes before the door closed, keeping him momentarily at bay.

"Guys?" Never in her life had their faces been more dear to her. "I'm in big trouble. We've got to get out of here now! I'll tell you about it when we're in the taxi." She removed the robe and wet sundress.

"They only have chauffeur driven cars here at the hotel."

"Well *we're* going to call for a taxi. Will one of you do it please?" she begged. "Tell them to be here in fifteen minutes."

"Where are we going in such an all-fired hurry?"

"Across the border to France. We'll drive to the nearest airport and take the first flight leaving for anywhere that puts as much distance as possible between us and hi— Italy," she amended.

"You've got to be kidding."

She shook her damp head at Olivia.

"I've seen that look before. She's not kidding," Piper whispered. They followed her to the bathroom. "Does this have something to do with what happened today when the police kept us so long?"

"No." She removed her watch, then her necklace, her skin still seemed to burn where he'd kissed her.

"I detect the scent of a man."

At Olivia's adroit surmise, a distinct blush covered every particle of Greer's skin. She was thankful for the protection of the elaborate sculptured design on the glass shower door, although it reminded her of the one on the floor of the pool.

*The floor she never got to inspect at close range because she was snatched away by a force that still caused her to tremble.*

"I didn't think there was a man alive who could make you run."

"If you must know, I tangled with a shark."

"In the pool?" Piper blurted incredulously.

"This one had arms and legs..." And a masculine appeal that ought to be banned from existence Greer groaned inwardly as she washed the suds out of her hair.

"Did he manhandle you?"

She reached for the tap to shut off the water. "Not exactly."

"Then he threatened you."

Greer shivered. "Not in so many words."

"If you expect us to check out of the hotel tonight when we've only had a couple of hours sleep, then you'd better tell us everything first."

Olivia was right.

After they left the bathroom, Greer grabbed two fluffy towels. With one encircling her head, the other fastened around her body, she padded in the other room after them.

Her sisters sat on their own beds cross-legged, waiting

for her. She sank down on the side of hers. "I—I have this horrible feeling I'm not only in over my head, but there could be serious consequences. It's my own fault of course."

She jumped to her feet, unable to relax. "In the beginning, the idea of turning the tables on an honest to goodness European playboy sounded very fun and challenging. That was until—"

"Until you met up with a real one tonight," Piper supplied.

Greer nodded jerkily. "There was this black-haired Adonis in the pool who would put any Olympic swimmer to shame. When he got out—"

Images flashed before Greer's eyes. She couldn't believe such an attractive man existed.

"Since you can't find the words, we get the picture." Olivia steepled her fingers. "Did he throw you in the pool without your permission?"

Her face went scarlet. "No."

Piper leaned forward. "Did you fall in by accident?"

"No! It was nothing like that," she confessed in a quieter tone.

"Then what *was* it like?"

"If you must know, he took one look at the pendant and asked me to swim with him. Everything happened just as we planned it back in Kingston. There was this gorgeous playboy who knew who the Duchess of Colorno was. He came on to me because of the pendant."

"So you just jumped in the pool with him?" By now their eyes had rounded.

"The Duchess girls don't jump, remember?"

Olivia's mouth broke into a grin. "Of course not. Still wearing your clothes, you executed one of your graceful dives to make certain you captured his attention."

"I guess," came her muffled admission.

Laughter filled the room, but Greer didn't join in. It was something they noticed.

"So what happened next?" Piper urged her to keep talking.

Greer kneaded her hands convulsively. "That's when everything went wrong."

"What did he do? Come on," Olivia prodded. "Let's hear it all, no matter how embarrassing it might be. Otherwise we won't know how much trouble you're really in."

"It's bad," she whispered. "Trust me."

That wiped the smiles off their lovely faces. "He didn't—"

"No—" Greer blurted. "But he *could* have done anything. My dress was floating around my waist and he was so powerful and so...so—" Heat suffused her face.

Piper slid off the bed. "And you think that if you'd been alone with him, he would have taken advantage of you whether you told him no or not?"

She drew in a sharp breath. "What I think is, that man goes *where* he wants, *when* he wants, and does *whatever* he wants. Period. The pendant seemed to have particular significance for him."

In the next breath she told them about the conversation in the pool, leaving out the parts about both kisses which were too personal. They'd shaken her so badly she couldn't discuss it, not even with her sisters.

"What's his name?"

"I have no idea."

Olivia rolled her eyes. "Greer—"

"I know," she muttered in self-deprecation, rubbing her arms nervously. "It gets worse. I tried to outbluff him by pretending that I wasn't in the most compromising position of my life. I flirted a little before telling him I wouldn't be in Genoa after tomorrow because we were going to Vernazza.''

"You *told* him we were going there?''

"I'm a fool, Piper, and I know it, b-but that was before I realized how dangerous he was. And after what he said about a secret grotto and the sun and the sand and me rising *au naturel* from a seashell, my gut instinct says he'll follow me there with the excuse he wanted to give me back my shoes.''

After his words to her at the door, Greer just *knew* he was the type of man that would turn up again.

"It sounds thrilling to me,'' Piper murmured.

Olivia nodded. "Me, too.''

"Guys—'' Greer cried in sheer panic, "this man *invented* the double-entendre. He's…dangerous.''

"You're saying that because you've never met anyone so gorgeous in your life, and you don't know how to handle your attraction to him.''

"I'm not attracted, Piper!''

"Yes, you are,'' Olivia contradicted her.

"All right. But even if I am, he's the kind of man who's off-limits!'' her voice shook. "When we decided to spend the Husband Fund, we should have stuck to the movie version we saw in Mr. Carlson's office and targeted sensible men. It would have been a lot safer than making ourselves the targets to wealthy playboys.''

Olivia frowned. "Our plan worked in theory. You're just not used to Italian men. It's perfectly natural for him to have been forward with you. It's the way they're made.''

"Olivia's right,'' Piper backed her sister up. "After all, you are very beautiful, Greer. Don can't ever take his eyes off you, but he's American, and American males aren't as obvious. Look how long it took him to make his first move toward you.''

"Try six months," Olivia drawled. "Greer—maybe this stranger *is* totally unscrupulous. Then again, maybe he isn't. You haven't given him enough of a chance yet to find out."

"You had to be there, Olivia!" Greer snapped.

"Not necessarily. You said he has black hair. With you being so blond, and having the most unusual violet eyes, it's no surprise he was drawn to you. I noticed a ton of men staring at you all day today. He couldn't help himself any more than they could. You *did* say he restrained himself."

Heat crept over Greer's body. "Not completely," she finally admitted. "He kissed me in the pool, a-and at the door."

"I thought so," Olivia murmured.

"Did you kiss him back?" Piper prodded.

"Of course not! H-he didn't kiss my lips."

Her sisters eyed each other before Piper said, "That explains everything."

"What do you mean?" Greer fired back.

"You're a take-charge kind of woman. He knew that and found his way around you. Sounds like you'll be getting a marriage proposal out of him before long."

"I don't want a marriage proposal. I just want to get away from him. Maybe we should just go home."

"We will, *after* our vacation is over," Olivia placated her. "Since we've already paid the money for the boat and can't get it back, I say we put the pendants away, drop the Duchess act and enjoy the rest of our trip like any normal tourists."

"I second the motion," Piper concurred.

"But I already told the stranger I was related to the Duchess of Colorno."

"It's too late to worry about the fact that we made reservations for the boat in the name of the Duchess of

Kingston," Olivia advised. "We just won't pull it on any-one else we meet."

"You're overreacting. However if or when Signore Mysterioso does show up," she mimicked Greer's pronun-ciation, "and you still want protection, he'll have to deal with all three of us."

"That's right," Piper chimed in. "Should he come around, we won't let you out of our sight for a single second. How does that sound?"

"In theory, it sounds fine."

"Good. Now that we've got everything settled, let's go to bed and sleep in until they throw us out. Okay?"

"Okay..." Greer's voice trailed, not nearly as confi-dent.

Within a few minutes the lights had been extinguished and everyone had crawled under their covers. Soon Greer could tell her sisters were dead to the world.

It took a lot longer for her to succumb to the fatigue draining her body. That was because neither Olivia nor Piper had ever been stalked by a shark.

She kept feeling the spots where his mouth had scorched her throat and neck, imagining he'd actually taken little bites out of her.

"Nic? It's Max. I've got Luc on the line with me so we can have a three-way conference call."

"Luc?"

"I'm here, Nic. Good to hear your voice."

"It's like old times."

Max's two cousins, Nic and Luc, the son's of his fa-ther's sisters, were as close to him as brothers.

One aunt had married Carlos de Pastrana from Marbella, Spain. The other was married to Jean-Louis de Falcon from Monaco. All three parents were the direct descen-dants of the House of Parma-Bourbon and had married royalty. Max felt as at home at their residences as they felt at the Varano villa in Colorno.

Being between the ages of thirty-three and thirty-four, the Varano cousins had spent every possible moment together growing up, be it at school or on vacation. But five months ago tragedy struck, killing Nic's fiancée and almost causing Luc to lose his leg.

The accident had robbed both cousins of the joie de vivre Max had thought inherent in their natures. Much as he hated to admit it, he, too, had been in a state of despondency even before the ghastly accident. As far as he was concerned, if the three of them weren't careful, depression would turn them into old men before their time.

He could use their company right now and was glad for any excuse to bring them together.

"Forgive me for calling both of you at one in the morning, but this is important."

"What do you mean forgive?" Nic fired back. "As I recall, I kept you up half the night for weeks after the accident."

"And you spent the other half in my hospital room," Luc reminded him. "Hearing your voice is like a much-longed-for blast of fresh air. Especially when all I do lately is go from bed to work, to physical therapy, and then back to bed again."

"I couldn't agree more with Luc," Nic assured Max. "Thank God you've called. Tell us what you need and you've got it!"

Max was going to hold Nic to that. "Do you two think you could give me about ten days of your time?"

"Starting when?" they both demanded with such telltale eagerness, Max had his answer. Gripping the phone tighter he said, "In about six hours from now. It'll be a reunion *I've* needed."

Hard to believe there was a time when the three of them

had been young, inseparable *and* immortal. They hadn't believed the problems of ordinary men would ever touch their lives.

"You want us to join you in Colorno?"

Encouraged by Nic's question he said, "No. Vernazza, aboard the *Piccione*. I need you to help me crew."

Luc made a gruntlike sound. "With this damn cane, I'm afraid cooking is the only thing I'm good for at the moment."

"You're reading my mind, Luc. Since you're still out of commission, that's the job I'm assigning you. As we've learned from past experience, if preparing meals was left to me or Nic, we'd all starve to death. Nic can play captain."

"How come the *Piccione*?" Nic wanted to know. "You gave your boat to Fabio Moretti a couple of years ago."

"That's true, and it's his by right. I received the last payment on it several months ago."

"Good for him." A pregnant silence ensued. "So, I used to be fairly adept at reading your mind, but this time I have to admit you've got me baffled. What's going on?"

"Where are the Morettis going to be?" Luc asked.

"On an unexpected paid vacation."

"I take it this is some kind of emergency."

An image of the bewitching creature wearing what looked like their family's prized pendant flashed through Max's mind.

Her gorgeous eyes could have been spilled drops from those very amethysts. He pursed lips that could still feel and taste the flawless, perfumed skin where her life's blood throbbed close to the surface.

"I'm not sure what it is, Luc. But I know one thing. We have to strike now."

"Strike? That sounds cryptic."

"We may have our first break in discovering the person,

or persons, behind the theft of the family jewelry collection.''

An expletive came out of Luc. ''My parents never stop talking about it.''

''Nor mine,'' Nic murmured. ''Just before I left Marbella for the bankers' conference in Luxembourg, I heard Mama complaining to Papa because the head of security hasn't come up with a single lead in the case. As far as I'm concerned it's like we all said. Long ago the family jewels were removed from their settings and are sitting in someone's strong box.''

*Or around the delectable neck of an American vixen without scruples.*

''It might interest you to know that yesterday morning Signore Galli, the head of security at Genoa airport, detained three American women on entry because they were each wearing the Duchesse pendant.''

After a collective silence, ''There's only *one* pendant!'' Then they exploded with laughter.

That had been Max's first reaction, too. The jewelry collection was one of Italy's greatest treasures. Whoever stole it from the ducal palace in Colorno was the object of an intensive search.

For over a year now Italy's top investigators in conjunction with the CIA, Scotland Yard and Interpol had been working on the case without success.

''This Signore Galli's eyesight must be impaired.''

''I don't know, Nic. The Duchesse pendant I saw a little while ago looked like the genuine article.''

Quiet reigned once more.

''You *saw* one of the pendants they were wearing?''

''I did, Luc. Up close and very personal, if you know what I mean.''

The inference that Max had been with one of the females wearing it didn't escape his cousins who after another telling silence urged him to explain everything.

"These women, Greer, Piper and Olivia, are extremely beautiful, twenty-seven-year-old blond triplets."

"Triplets?"

"*Si.* Not identical up close. Together they make an amazing sight. Their passports say their last name is Duchess. They live in Kingston, New York.

"I found out they were planning to go sailing from Vernazza later today. According to Fabio's records, the person who chartered the *Piccione* called herself the Duchess of Kingston from the House of Parma-Bourbon."

His cousins' sounds of disbelief rattled the phone line.

"I did a little homework and discovered through an impeccable source there is no such Kingston title in existence today."

"Which sister thought up the idea of capitalizing on such a blatant piece of fiction?" Nic demanded.

"I have no idea," Max muttered. "Greer claimed her ancestor was the Duchess of Colorno."

"*Incroyable!*" Luc bit out.

"I agree the whole situation sounds unbelievable. I wouldn't have taken any stock in Signore Galli's report if I hadn't followed the three of them from the Splendido to the San Giorgio church and back. They were each wearing a matching pendant. It's anyone's guess why, especially in light of the theft."

"Why would they enter the scene of the crime wearing copies of the genuine article unless they wanted to be caught for some reason?"

"I don't know, Nic. Perhaps it's an elaborate joke perpetrated by the thieves to rub it in the family's face that we'll never find out who was responsible."

"Or, it's possible one of the pendants they're wearing

*is* the genuine article and they're bargaining for bigger stakes,'' Luc muttered.

"My sentiments exactly. To make this even more interesting Greer claimed they were in Italy visiting their... relatives.''

"Relatives—'' Nic blurted. "*We're* the relatives.''

"Exactly. Under the circumstances I thought you and Luc would like to help me facilitate a meeting between long lost cousins.''

"Go on,'' Nic urged. At this point Max had garnered his cousins' undivided attention.

"We need to find out who they really are, why they're here. Are they acting alone? If not, who sent them? What is their agenda? The only way to get that kind of information is to use the old-fashioned method of extracting information, if you know what I mean,'' he drawled. "I trust you two haven't lost your touch.''

"I like the idea of six 'kissing cousins' very much,'' Luc said, easily reading Max's mind. "There's no place cozier than the *Piccione* for what you're suggesting.''

"Agreed. While we're crewing, we'll do everything we can to get their undivided attention. Here's my plan. Nic? When Fabio first brings them aboard, I want you to keep them entertained while I go through their luggage and steal the pendants.

"We'll sail for Lerici. After dinner I'll take them on a tour of the castle. That will give you and Luc time to fly to Parma by helicopter, show the pendants to Signore Rossi for examination, and be back on board the *Piccione* before my return with our guests.

"Depending on what we learn about the pendants, we'll know if we need more time to get information out of these women, or call in the police immediately and have them arrested.''

Low laughter rumbled out of Nic. It was the first genuine emotion Max had heard from his cousin since the funeral, a sure indication he wasn't completely dead of feeling after all.

For that matter, Luc actually sounded excited about something which was a huge change from his brooding apathy of late. Both cousins' reactions constituted a plus Max hadn't counted on.

"I'll be honest and admit I'm looking forward to spending quality time getting as close as possible to Greer Duchess." In fact Max was living in anticipation. After tasting the satiny skin of her neck and throat, not once but twice, he'd developed an instantaneous addiction for her he needed to satisfy before the day was out.

"I'll meet you at the boat at seven," Luc declared.

"What about you, Nic?" After losing his fiancée, Nic hadn't looked at another woman.

"I'll be there."

Good. Better than good. Nic had been in hibernation long enough. "I've a feeling this is going to be like old times. *Ciao.*"

The brochure described Vernazza as a jewel. But the picture of it hadn't in any way prepared Greer to appreciate its spectacular beauty. The only natural port village of five towns making up Cinque Terre had a cut and polish like no stone she'd ever seen.

As she took in the brilliant facets of tower-shape houses clustered in different levels against the steep cliffs, the stark blue clarity of sea and sky made her eyes water.

She gasped at the range of color pitting forest and emerald-green mountains against the yellow, pink and rose of the more elaborate palaces and castles decorated by portals and porticos.

The delighted sighs coming from her sisters bespoke their mutual entrancement of this Mediterranean masterpiece the Genoese had protected against barbarians and Saracens centuries earlier.

Greer longed to hike the narrow paths climbing dizzily from the small square up the rocky face. But she would have to explore the town and hidden Vernazzola stream at the end of their trip because they were already late to board the sailboat.

Due to the thousands of tourists flocking to the Riviera for the Grand Prix, there was a lineup at the train station for tickets. As a result, Greer and her sisters didn't reach the stone jetty of Vernazza's small harbor until three in the afternoon, three hours past the appointed time.

A dozen or more boats in various colors were moored on the sheltered side of the dancing blue water. But there was only one catamaran. It stood out from the others like white chalk on a new blackboard.

She couldn't wait until they were at sea.

Though the haunting stranger from last night hadn't been waiting outside her hotel room door this morning with her shoes, or accosted her in the lobby when they'd checked out of the Splendido, *or* shown up at the dock, she still didn't feel safe.

Something about him had threatened her peace of mind in more ways than she could explain, even to her sisters. Given the slightest opportunity, she feared he might just devour her whole. Mind, body, soul, psyche—all of her...gone.

It was an absurd notion of course. He couldn't really do that, yet until the boat left the harbor, she wouldn't be able to breathe normally.

*"Buon giorno, signorine,"* a male voice sounded behind them. Greer jumped in reaction, fearing the worst. "I'm Fabio Moretti, the owner of the *Piccione*. Welcome to Vernazza."

She heard her sisters introduce themselves. Piper gave

her a nudge. With her breath still trapped in her lungs, Greer turned around.

Relief swamped her to discover a smiling, dark blond Italian of medium height wearing blue trousers and a darker blue sport shirt. His hazel eyes gave them an admiring glance before he shook hands with them.

"Which one of you is the Duchess of Kingston?"

"We all are," Olivia declared. Greer moaned inwardly.

He tugged on his earlobe. "Ah, because you are—how do you say it? Treeplets. *Capisce!*" His head reared back in understanding.

Piper nodded. "But as we indicated in our e-mail, we'd like that kept confidential."

"Of course. Just so you know, I arranged for a special chef for your trip. He has cooked for several royals of the House of Parma-Bourbon. Right now he's busy in the galley preparing dinner. You are in for a very special treat while you sail on the *Piccione.*"

Greer eyed her sisters in consternation before she looked back at him. "You didn't need to go to all that trouble, *signore.*"

"It was my pleasure. Though the people of Vernazza are Ligurians, the Duchy of Parma holds a special place in our hearts, mine in particular. If you'll follow me below, I'll introduce you to the captain who's anxious to get underway.

"Don't worry about your bags. The first mate will bring them to your staterooms. He'll be your steward and go through the boat safety drill with you once you've cast off. Shall we board?"

They stepped off the dock onto the boat and started up the side stairs after him. At this point Greer was feeling horribly guilty over the whole Duchess deception and knew her sisters were, too.

Under other circumstances she would have loved to chat

with Signore Moretti, a local who might be able to shed light on the story about the Duchess and her progeny. But at this juncture Greer realized it wouldn't be prudent for several reasons.

His boat more than lived up to her expectations, diverting her attention for the moment. Not only did it feel like an elegant luxury apartment at sea, but it came loaded with a wind glider, snorkeling gear, fishing gear, water skis, knee boards, sun mattresses… Anything and everything to ensure a dream vacation.

Then Greer caught sight of a striking, thirtyish looking male in sunglasses coming out the crew's quarters at the head.

Because of his well-defined physique visible beneath the indigo T-shirt and white cargo pants he was wearing, he bore a superficial resemblance to the tall stranger from the Splendido.

Her heart rose in her throat. But when he joined them in the main saloon where there was more light, she realized her mistake.

This man's hair was straighter in texture and had brown highlights among the black. His rugged features put her in mind of the group of proud, handsome Castilians who'd flirted with them on the train as it had passed through one tunnel after another.

The owner of the boat said something to him in Italian. When he removed his glasses, she found herself looking into black fringed eyes the color of rich brown loam.

"*Buenas tardes, señoritas.* My name is Nicolas, but please call me Nic. We are always informal on the *Piccione.*"

A gorgeous Spaniard who knew it, and spoke Italian and English, too. Impressive. Greer had been right about his origins.

Everyone said hello.

"It is indeed a pleasure to sail a boat with three such breathtaking sisters who look alike, yet are so different." His gaze traveled over each of them, but seemed to rest on Piper the longest. "Forgive me for staring, *señorita…?*"

"Piper."

*"Piperrre…"* He seemed to relish rolling her name across his tongue. "Your eyes are the same rare hue as the aquamarine waters along the Riviera di Ponente. *Muy muy bella.*"

Piper did have remarkable eyes. The trail of men who'd looked into them and been smitten was miles long. Obviously she didn't have to wear the Duchesse pendant to attract this man's attention.

Not for the first time did Greer regret last night's reckless, impulsive, unquestionably dangerous escapade.

"Thank you."

"We're sorry we're late," Olivia inserted.

"No problem, *señorita…?*"

"My name's Olivia."

He flashed her a seductive smile. It seemed not only Italian men, but all European men in general, had a way of invading a woman's space like nobody else, giving her no breathing room whatsoever.

To Greer's chagrin she discovered their captain, like the dark-haired stranger from last night, had the kind of overwhelming good looks you didn't run into every day, or every year. Or possibly never.

"As I was saying, *señoritas,* do not be concerned about the time. This is the busiest season of the year and delays on land are routine. That is the beauty of traveling by water. When there's no wind to fill the sails, we have engine power to take us where we want to go. I know places where we can be virtually alone."

Greer tensed at the unmistakable innuendo. "All we require is that you follow the itinerary we worked out with Signore Moretti.''

She felt his slight hesitation before he said, ''Naturally, *señorita.*'' The assurance rolled off his liquid tongue, almost as if he'd sensed her misgivings and could read her mind. Almost as if he was mocking her. ''But we will make one slight exception.''

Greer *knew* it!

''Before we dock at Monterosso tonight, I thought you might enjoy a visit to the port town of Lerici. There's a castle you should see.''

When Greer didn't say anything, Piper filled in the uncomfortable silence. ''That sounds exciting.''

Normally it would have sounded exciting to her, too, but for some reason she couldn't shake, Greer wasn't sure she trusted the captain completely.

''I don't remember hearing your name, *señorita.*''

Really. It was on the tip of her tongue to play the same game the stranger had played with her last night and ask the captain to guess, but she restrained herself. ''It's Greer.''

She saw intelligence reflected in those dark brown eyes studying her with such unusual intensity it made her suspicious. Perhaps it was her imagination, but the captain still reminded her a little of the stranger from last night.

''Greer is an obscure yet charming diminutive of Gregorio, the first Greek pope, yet you all have the gilt-blond hair of the Saxons,'' he observed. ''Why were you not given commensurate names?''

Commensurate? Who *was* this man?

''If our mother were alive, you could ask her.'' Ignoring her sisters' frowns she said, ''If you'll excuse us, we'd like to freshen up.''

Signore Moretti who'd been oddly silent throughout their exchange said, ''There are three staterooms ready for you with your own queen-size beds and private bathrooms. Before I leave you in Nic's capable hands, allow me to show you.''

Without casting another glance at the captain, Greer took the lead behind the owner of the *Piccione*. Her sisters might be blinded by the captain's charm, but Greer wasn't!

For a seaman, he possessed an amazing grasp of etymology. Too amazing in her opinion. She felt like they'd jumped out of one proverbial frying pan into a fire where things were threatening to get a lot hotter.

As if to add to her concerns, their plan never to be separated was foiled when she realized the light, airy staterooms were located in three different corners of the catamaran.

Each one contained fabulous oversize baskets of flowers, fruit and chocolates, plus a well stocked minifridge with every kind of drink from mineral water to soda and wine.

Everything was lovely. She had no complaints.

But by the time Signore Moretti had wished them a happy trip and disappeared, she had the premonition something was wrong. When she detected vibrations running through her feet, she jumped. They were moving!

It was too late to get off.

# CHAPTER FOUR

PIPER SIGHED. "I think Vernazza is more beautiful than Portofino, if that's possible."

Greer's sisters had scrambled on top of the bed and were looking out the porthole at the receding harbor.

"Admit the captain's the most beautiful man you've ever laid eyes on."

Greer knew of one exception to Olivia's observation, but she wisely chose to remain quiet on that subject. "Don't get too excited about him," she cautioned.

They both swung around, darting her a vexed glance. "What's wrong with you?" Piper chided.

Olivia folded her arms. "You were rude to him a few minutes ago, you know."

"That's because something about him doesn't ring true."

"For heaven sake's, Greer. Just because he's attractive doesn't make him a predator."

"I'm not talking about his looks, though they are exceptional. It's his whole demeanor. Your eyes, Señorita *Piperrre*—" She did a faithful representation of the captain. "They are like aquamarine waters. Your name, Señorita Greer, is obscure yet *charming*— My gosh— The man's a menace!"

Piper grinned. "You mean he reminds you of the way the stranger talked to you last night. I thought we decided that European males come on to women much more directly, so we just have to learn to deal with it."

"Piper's right," Olivia argued. "The captain may be Spanish, but they all have Mediterranean blood flowing

57

through their veins. It makes them different from the men we're used to dating.''

''I don't know, guys. I've a feeling our captain plays by a set of rules we've never heard of.''

''That's what you said about Signore Mysterioso.''

''They remind me of each other.''

''Greer—do you have any idea how paranoid you sound?''

''*He's* the one who sounds too educated to be doing work like this. If he were a real sea captain, he would be running a naval vessel or a passenger ship or something.''

Olivia hunched her shoulders. ''Maybe he does this for fun when he's on vacation. What do we care? We came to the Riviera for ten days of fun, plus the hope of meeting some authentic playboys.''

Greer shook her head. ''Technically we came with a definite plan to get them to *propose!*

''Can you honestly picture that three-tongued Don Juan above deck bringing himself to ask for a woman's hand in marriage? Even if he knew the Hope diamond could be his?'' she exploded.

''Probably not,'' Piper admitted. ''But then he's the captain, so he's not in the running.''

''Then somebody needs to tell him that. I saw the way he was devouring you with his eyes, as if you were a feast and he couldn't decide which dish to try first.''

''That stranger last night really freaked you out,'' Olivia said softly.

''The captain freaks me, too. Let's face it, guys. When we thought up our absurd plan, we'd just gotten home from Mr. Carlson's office. It was grief that made us delusional.

''I vote that when we dock at Monterossa tonight, we say 'thanks, but no thanks,' and head straight for the train station. I don't care if we have to stay there all night. Once we're back in Genoa, we'll wait on standby for a flight home.''

''Home?'' Piper's brows knit together. ''No way, Greer. It's too big a waste of Daddy's money.''

''We paid a trip cancellation fee,'' Greer reminded them. ''I say we ask for a refund. Of course we won't get all the money back, but it's better than nothing.''

''I came to see the Grand Prix.''

''I realize that, Olivia, but there'll be another car race next year. You can come again for the right reason, and on your own money. I just think we're in over our heads here.''

Olivia eyed her soberly. ''You're serious.''

Greer nodded. ''What kind of a vacation will it be if the whole time we're trying to have fun on this catamaran, we're fighting off a captain who thinks he's God's gift to women and believes we're titled and dripping in money and jewels? If you think Signore Moretti withheld that vital piece of information from his crew, then you'd believe we're sailing on the Caribbean!''

''You don't have to be sarcastic,'' Piper murmured, sounding hurt.

Olivia trained concerned eyes on her. ''With all of us protecting each other, the captain will be helpless to do anything, so I don't see the problem. It'll be three against one. If we stick together, he can't make a move we won't know about.''

''Don't be so sure. He's runs this boat. You heard him say he knew of places where we could be virtually alone. He wasn't kidding. We're out of our depth here. They're not ordinary men. They know how to seduce a woman.''

''Then we'll have to be on our guard.''

''You say that now, Piper, but they have ways of getting you to do things you never planned to do.''

Olivia drew closer. "Are you saying something else happened last night we don't know about?"

Greer's heart pounded in her ears. "No," she confessed shakily, "but—"

"But you think you won't be able to hold out against him if you were ever to see him again."

After her experience last night, she knew it would take a strong woman to resist a man like him or the captain and secretly she just didn't know if she could.

"Let's just say I don't want to find out." If she gave the dark stranger one inch, he'd take ten thousand miles. There would be a price to pay for carrying on a passionate ten-day affair with him. After it was over she would return home alone where she would stay in pain for the rest of her life.

No way... She was a Duchess, and a Duchess girl held out for marriage and everything that went with it.

"Guys—we've enjoyed our moment of insanity pretending to be duchesses. Now it's over."

"But not the whole trip." Piper stood firm. "We won't let the captain take advantage of any of us. We'll room together the whole time. One of those sun mattresses will work for an extra bed."

"I was just going to suggest it," Olivia murmured. "Now what do you say we go up on deck in a few minutes and enjoy the view until dinner? I don't know about you but I'm thrilled we have a French chef on board who'll guarantee us a fabulous meal."

To lighten the mood she handed everyone some chocolate and pears, one of their favorite fruits. "I figure we need a snack before the first mate gives us the boat drill."

"I just hope *he* isn't anothe—"

"Give it up, Greer!"

At Piper's admonition, Greer bowed her head, not wanting to entertain the possibility there could be another one like the shark from last night swimming anywhere loose around this boat.

It was such a troubling thought, she sat on the bed covered in a blue print spread and munched away. In a few minutes she got up to dispose of the wrappers and cores.

When she emerged from the spotless white bathroom loaded with all types of soaps, perfumes, lotions and shampoo, she announced, "I'm going to go to the stateroom on the other side of the boat where I saw my suitcase. I'll be right back with it."

"Mine's in the other one. I'll go with you," Olivia said. Together they slipped into the passageway and parted company by the stairs.

The vibrations had stopped, which meant it was the air in the sails, not the engine, that was propelling them. Greer loved the gentle rocking motion of the boat. Under other circumstances, this would have been the dream trip of a lifetime.

What an imbecile she'd been to touch the money their father had left them. They'd *all* been imbeciles. Look what had happened because they'd gone along with his ridiculous stipulation to try to find a husband!

Furious with herself, she flung open the door to the stateroom, which had been left unlocked. When she entered, she expected to see her suitcase on the floor, but it was nowhere to be found. The first mate must have put it in the closet. She crossed the expanse and opened it.

A surprised cry sprang from her lips to discover her clothes on hangers, her shoes neatly placed in separate compartments.

Her *gold* shoes.

Greer felt the blood drain from her face. There was the faint sound of a click behind her. She didn't have to turn around to know who was standing a few feet away, blocking her only escape route with the greatest of enjoyment.

*I know Vernazza well. Since you show no fear of the water, I would be happy to take you to a secret grotto, which can only be reached by swimming a short distance beneath the sea.*

*Noooooooooooo*— It couldn't be. She'd known he would show up at some point on their trip, but not as a member of the crew aboard the *Piccione*! This couldn't possibly be happening.

"*Buona sera,* Greer." His haunting voice sounded like the night breeze swishing through the cypress trees, carrying the scent of lemon and jasmine down to the sea.

"I couldn't sleep all night anticipating being with you again. It's the only reason I was able to let you slip away, although I'll admit I came close to carrying you down to the sea for a moonlight swim."

Get a grip, Greer.

You can't let him see what this has done to you. Brazen it out till later. Play it cool.

She could hear her father's encouraging whisper, "Play it like a Duchess."

The thought of her loving parent gave her the courage to turn around and present an imperious smile to the one man who could be her total ruination if she didn't put an ocean between them in the next eighteen hours.

She steeled herself not to react to the devastating sensuality he emitted wearing one of those short-sleeved black crew necks. He'd tucked it inside thigh-molding jeans that rode low on his incredible male body.

Greer flashed him an imperious smile. "*Buona sera, signore.* So the first mate is last night's man of mystery."

"Life plays many tricks, does it not?"

"How did you know I would be aboard the *Piccione*?"

"As soon as you told me you were coming to Vernazza, I asked a close friend of mine to keep an eye out for you. It must be fate that brought us together without my having

He cocked his head. "You didn't answer my question. Tell me more about the Italian side of your family. You have me completely enchanted, Greer. I want to learn everything about you."

Everything?

Beneath the ardency of his words she could tell he was driven by a curiosity separate from his desire for her. Of what real interest could Greer's roots be to him?

She gave him the benefit of a full, unguarded smile. "I'm afraid I left little to the imagination when I joined you in the pool. You've already learned I can be impulsive, and that I love to swim.

"Isn't it nice that in this new century, the working class can enjoy their time off at the Splendido in exactly the same way as the aristocracy?"

She'd posed the question while he pulled a life jacket from the footlocker.

He flashed her a mystifying smile. "That all depends on what you mean by enjoy. The worker is there on borrowed time and limited funds which adds a certain...edge to the experience." He moved toward her.

The first mate exuded an urbane sophistication that sat at odds with the kind of job he did. He seemed too powerful a personality, too shrewd and intelligent to take orders from anyone else.

Though he appeared perfectly at home on the boat, she was convinced he ruled another world apart from this one.

"I wouldn't know."

"Who could blame you. After all, you were born to be the Duchess of Kingston."

Though his silky observation had sounded totally offhand, Greer had the sudden revelation he was after her for whatever he could get out of her. Money...jewels...her virtue.

It shouldn't have shocked her. This was what she and

her sisters had hoped would happen when they came to the Riviera. But now that he was calling her bluff in earnest, the charade no longer felt like a joke.

To hide her dismay, she gave a careless shrug of her feminine shoulders, drawing his attention to the periwinkle silk blouse that crisscrossed the bodice.

His bold gaze dropped from her curves to the wide belt cinching her waist. By the time his eyes took in the line of her matching skirt which flowed from the flare of womanly hips, he'd managed to squeeze every ounce of breath from her lungs.

"It seems criminal to have to cover up what nature has so exquisitely endowed." Without asking her permission, he helped her into the jacket and secured the front straps.

After the way she'd plunged into the water at the hotel, she supposed he had every reason to believe she'd thrown maidenly virtue out the window long ago.

Little did he know her primal instinct was to slap his face. For the moment, all she could do was keep up the pretense until she could get away from him.

Restraining herself she said, "Seeing you busy like this at your job helps me understand why you were solicitous of my needs last night. Even to the point of returning my shoes? Has anyone ever told you *you* would make an excellent personal valet?"

With those words, she thought his patrician jaw hardened just a trifle. "No. You're the first. Are you offering me a full-time job?"

"Would you take it?"

"I would for the right price and benefits."

Her pulses throbbed. "I'll bet you're expensive."

"But that wouldn't be a problem for you."

"You mean because I'm a duchess?"

His lips twisted in a subtle smile. "Some titles have no money or property to back them up. But the pendant you were wearing last night tells me you can afford my exclusive services.''

It all got down to the pendant.

''Ah, but for how long?'' she asked with great daring.

''For as long as we continue to desire each other.''

Her body trembled. ''I'm afraid you misunderstood me. I was talking about valet service only.''

''So was I. Shall we test out one of my duties to see if my work measures up to your expectations?''

In the space of a millisecond he'd tugged on the straps he'd been tying so that she fell against his hard, powerful body. Without the life jacket separating them, her heart would have jammed into his.

His other hand cupped the back of her head where the gossamer strands brushed his fingers. He had the kind of strength that made it impossible for her to evade the insistent pressure of his male mouth. She was prepared to fight him with all her might.

But when that mouth closed inexorably over hers, he didn't swallow her alive in one gulp as she'd feared. Rather he played with her lips, nibbled on them, tasted them slowly, each time coaxing them farther apart, a little more and a little more.

After their exciting verbal skirmish, she felt a seductive rhythm building like the flow of the tide, racing up the beach a little higher, a little stronger. It filled all the aching spaces in her body which yearned toward him of its own volition.

His mouth created such sweet ecstasy, pleasure pains never before awakened came alive, demanding assuagement from the source that created them.

The moans she heard turned out to be her own.

Moans of need, of desire she didn't know she could feel. She felt helpless, beautiful. Alive. She didn't know herself anymore. He was making her feel immor—

"Greer?"

Olivia's voice.

The door flew open. "Quick! We've got some—Greer!"

Piper's shocked cry reverberated in the cabin.

Greer wrenched her lips from the man who'd been kissing her into oblivion and turned around in guilty reaction, but her senses were reeling.

Ironically her captor had to be the one to steady her in his strong arms. It would take time to recover from an experience that had been a breathtaking education in what really went on between a man and woman.

*"Buona sera, signorine."*

"What's going on?" Olivia demanded in a quiet, yet chilling voice. Piper looked ready to tackle him to the ground. Greer didn't know her siblings could be this fierce.

Of course they wouldn't have had any success if they'd tried to restrain him. The fact that he ignored their edicts and still held her arms firmly in his grasp testified to that truth.

"I-it isn't what you think," Greer stammered. "You've misinterpreted what was happening."

"That's right," he said in a suave tone. "Your sister and I were getting…reacquainted. Last night there was so little time before she ran off to bed, leaving me desolate."

Her chest heaved.

"Olivia? Piper?" Every breath sounded ragged, even to her own ears. "T-this is the man I met at the Splendido last night."

After the way she'd carried on about him earlier, she couldn't believe she was defending him now. However she drew the line at accusing him of a crime her sisters assumed would have taken place if they hadn't barged in.

To her shame, nothing had gone on she hadn't let happen and he knew it!

The truth was, it had given her a perverse thrill to spar with him. She'd loved baiting him. The last thing on her mind had been to scream her head off at the first sight of him so her sisters would come running.

When they recalled this incident later, they would have to admit she hadn't been struggling with him. Au contraire. She'd ended up being an eager participant.

That's what was so mortifying—to realize how completely out of control she'd been the second his mouth had covered hers.

He'd kissed her as if he were starving for her. Admittedly she'd kissed him back with a matching hunger that seemed to have come out of nowhere and sought appeasement only he could give.

Who knew how long their passionate interlude might have gone on if her prolonged absence hadn't prompted her sisters to come in search of her? She had only herself to blame for this latest disaster.

Piper made no move to leave. "Aren't you going to introduce us?"

"I don't believe we caught his name," Olivia murmured.

A betraying blush crept into Greer's cheeks.

"Allow me to do the honors," said the man whose mouth had done things that were still sending out shock waves to the tiniest follicle of her body.

"I'm Max, the first mate on the *Piccione*. I saw the three of you out walking last night. It was a beautiful sight, one I'll never forget."

His hands caressed her arms down to the fingertips, then relinquished them. While Greer continued to tremble in reaction, he'd reached the open doorway in a few athletic strides.

Before disappearing he said, "*Signorine?* Meet me on

deck in five minutes with the life jackets you'll find in the footlockers of your staterooms. I'll show you how to fasten them correctly. Knowing what to do will save your lives if, heaven forbid, there should be an emergency on board.''

# CHAPTER FIVE

IN THE wake of his departure, Greer realized an explanation was in order. She blurted, "What you saw was nothing more than the result of my insulting him. Rather than fight him, I decided it might be wiser to let him get it out of his system."

To her surprise, her sisters shut the door, then put a finger to their lips.

"What's wrong?" Greer whispered.

"Just listen," Piper whispered back. "Our pendants are gone." Greer blinked. "We discovered them missing while we were putting everything away in the drawers of our stateroom.

"I only opened my cosmetic bag to get out some sunscreen. That's when I noticed the pendant wasn't there. I asked Olivia to look in her bag thinking maybe I'd put it there by mistake last night, but hers was gone, too."

"Since our bags never left our sight after we packed them this morning, it means the members of the crew have to be jewel thieves who believe they've stolen a small fortune," Olivia surmised. "Do you still have yours?"

Did she?

Galvanized into action, Greer ran to the bathroom where the first mate had put her cosmetic bag. She opened it and found the little case she kept it in. The pendant winked up at her.

"Mine's still here," she said in shaky voice. "He was probably in the process of stealing it when I surprised him by accident."

The three of them stared at each other before Olivia said

to Greer, "We thought you were overreacting earlier, but now we know your premonitions have been right about everything."

Piper had a far away look in her eye. "For the stranger you met last night to show up today claiming to be the first mate, and then for us to discover him kissing you like there's no tomorrow, it's obvious something out of the ordinary is going on here, even if you are fatally attracted to him."

Fatally attracted. That's what it felt like.

A shiver chased across her skin. "I knew it couldn't be a coincidence. Remember my telling you how drawn he was to the pendant?"

"Yes. If all he'd wanted was to get you into bed, he probably could have managed that last night."

"Thanks for the vote of confidence, Olivia," Greer said before averting her eyes.

"We saw you in his arms just now," Piper pointed out. "You were hardly fighting him off. No one's blaming you. Good grief. He looks like a god, and it's perfectly evident he's attracted to you, as well. But he has come on way too strong, too fast! As for the captain, you were right about him. He's— He's—"

Greer groaned. "I know what you're trying to say." She took a deep breath. "Let's face it. Signore Moretti has an interesting little operation going here. It might be legitimate, but he gets lots of perks when idiots like us charter his boat pretending to be something we're not. We don't have anyone else to blame but ourselves for our loss. If the parents knew…"

"We can't think about that right now." Olivia glanced at her watch. "The first mate said five minutes. If you're up not on deck in about twenty seconds, he'll use that excuse to come down and find you. I suggest we hustle topside on the double, pretend nothing's wrong, and talk about what we're going to do later.''

"Agreed."

In the next breath they hurried to the other stateroom for more life jackets, then emerged into the dazzling late-afternoon sun for which the Riviera was famous.

A mild breeze filled the sails imprinted with a stylized pigeon in flight. It propelled the boat away from the post-card perfect coast receding farther into the distance.

"Signorine?"

Every time Greer heard the deep resonance of the first mate's voice, a current of electricity traveled through her body igniting her nervous system. Except that this time she was on to him and the captain. They'd been in the cockpit, talking. Plotting...

Some job those two had.

She wondered how many hundreds of wealthy women over the years, married or not, had been swept away by their amazing looks and overpowering charisma, never to be the same again. Never to recover their jewels again.

Science hadn't invented a vaccine to inoculate the female of the species against the invasion of such spectacular foreign male specimens. There was no known antidote. The best you could do was run for your life in the opposite direction and never look back!

That was exactly what she and her sisters intended to do tonight after they docked. Until then they would have to stick together like Vienna sausages in the can and bluff their way through this last poker game. Greer could only pray they escaped from their doomed adventure relatively unscathed.

As her nemesis approached, the devastating white smile he flashed convinced her he could read her mind. She avoided his gaze while he inspected the way her sisters had fastened their life jackets. Once he'd given them a few pointers, their drill began.

The boat and everything to do with it seemed to be a part of him, which ironically she had to admit was reassuring. In twenty minutes they knew where to find extra life buoys, a two-way radio, flares, fire extinguishers, an ax, sea rations, water, tool and first-aid kits, navigation lights, buckets, oars, the horn and a waterproof sea chart with compass.

"Do the two of you know how to swim as well as your sister?"

They nodded.

"Nevertheless you'll do exactly as I say when you're playing with any of the water gear. Even dive masters like myself or the other crew have to be prepared for the unexpected, so we'll obey the rules to the letter. Do you have any questions?"

Greer had one. "Why are we sailing in the opposite direction from Monterosso where we're docking this evening?"

She'd planned that part of the itinerary herself. Monterosso had the best beach of the Cinque Terre.

If this was going to be their last night in Italy, they would at least be able to tell their friends they'd bathed *once* in the waters of the Mediterranean.

His black eyes impaled her. "You're very astute to realize we've made a minor detour."

"You call 'due east' a minor detour, *signore?*"

His captivating smile might as well have caught hold of her heart and upended it. "Didn't the captain tell you we're making a stop at the port town of Lerici?"

"He mentioned it. What's so important?"

"A sixth century castle which is just magical. You and your sisters can explore to your heart's content."

What a bald lie! This was a setup he and the captain

had obviously worked out over years of enticing rich women. Drop the jewels off at Lerici, then proclaim innocence at a later date when it was discovered the pendants were missing.

The boat proved to be the perfect vehicle. Seduction on the high seas, their vulnerable captives at the mercy of their potent masculine appeal.

They had the moves and the jargon down so perfectly, they could do it in their sleep—read each other's minds without conversing! Greer could read the first mate's since it was as transparent as a bride's veil.

He thought himself as irresistible as Valentino, but he couldn't be more wrong. Though he'd shocked the daylights out of her with kisses that revealed her own sensuality—a sensuality she hadn't realized she possessed, it didn't mean she wanted to repeat the experience.

You only had to be scalded once to know you should stay away from boiling water.

"Since when does a captain take orders from his first mate?" she challenged him. "Surely as long as you're getting paid the going wage, your job has nothing whatsoever to do with the itinerary we decided on weeks ago."

Her attention was caught by his hands which opened, palms upward, in a gesture so typical of Italian men she couldn't look away.

"It was a mere suggestion, *signorina*."

*And I'm the Duchess of Kingston!*

"If we'd wanted to go on a tour of the paranormal, we would have started out in Transylvania."

His eyelids lowered to half mast. "It was very wise of you not to travel there. Even I, who do not have a drop of vampire blood in my veins, find it increasingly difficult to resist taking a bite out of you myself."

At the mention of the word "bite," the spot where he'd

kissed her neck beneath the pendant began throbbing again. She fought not to react.

On cue her instinct for self-preservation came to the fore. Her chin jutted. "You can inform the captain we're not interested. Unless there's something else you needed to tell us that could save our lives, we'll be resting in our cabin until dinner's served."

After delivering her exit line she started walking toward the stairs, all the while feeling his fiery black eyes on her retreating back.

"It's ready now," he called out unexpectedly. "The chef is waiting."

The girls followed her to the stateroom. "Let's eat so they don't suspect anything, then we'll decide what we're going to do about our situation," she whispered as they removed their life jackets.

By tacit agreement they moved to the saloon. It was nothing short of amazing to see how it had been transformed. The table with an alençon lace cloth had been set for three.

Greer noted the Waterford crystal, fine Limoges china and a centerpiece of roses in reds, pinks and yellow. Her mouth watered the second she detected the fragrance of a seafood dish escaping the covered tureen.

The door to the adjoining galley opened. They spied a cane before a lean, hard-muscled male emerged. He was dressed in jeans and a gray pullover with the sleeves shoved above the elbows.

When he lifted his head of short-cropped black hair, Greer looked into the face of an olive-skinned Mediterranean man who possessed the kind of dark, dashing looks that caused women to make utter fools of themselves! No one knew about that better than she did.

If he weren't leaning so heavily on his cane, he would probably be as tall as the two men on deck.

*"Bonsoir, mesdemoiselles."* His deep-set gray eyes assessed Greer and Piper before traveling to Olivia.

There was no attempt on his part to apologize for studying her. His intimate perusal of her face and figure was guaranteed to wring a blush from the most hardened female. Greer had to give her sister points for holding it back.

"You must be the one named after the *olivier.*"

"Then whoever told you that was misinformed," Olivia threw out with gratifying sangfroid.

She'd sensed this gorgeous hunk of male was no chef. Not for this boat or a royal family. If any member of this crew was legitimate, then Greer and her sisters were the three good fairies!

His mouth curved into a wicked smile, verifying Greer's suspicions. "I'm never wrong, *mademoiselle.*"

"Really," Olivia mocked. "Well unless you required a cane from birth, it appears you made a wrong move at least once in your life."

Whoa, Olivia!

His handsome face turned dark as a thunderhead, revealing a man who had a dangerous look now that Olivia had struck him where it hurt.

It was patently clear that not only had the spoils been equally divided ahead of time, she and her sisters were about to be served up for their captors' delectation.

Not if Greer could help it!

"Monsieur *Luc,* is it?" she addressed him in her best bad French. "I'm afraid there was a slight oversight on our part. We forgot to tell Signore Moretti we're allergic to fish."

"It's a shame," Piper played along. "How sad that the beautiful dinner you labored over so long with your bad leg has to go to waste."

On their way out of the saloon Olivia turned to him.

"What was it Marie Antoinette once said, 'If the passengers can't eat fish, let the crew eat it'?"

Bravo, Olivia!

They walked with great dignity to their stateroom. Once they'd locked the door behind them, Greer turned to her sisters. This time she was the one to put a finger to her lips. "We've been *had,* guys."

"Tell me about it!" Piper whispered furiously.

Olivia's angry brows knit together. "It all started when we were detained by the police at the Genoa airport. Three hours for what? In a matter of a minute we told them all we knew which was absolutely nothing!"

"And when I met the *first mate* at the Splendido it certainly wasn't by accident!" Greer muttered through gritted teeth. "When he called for a robe, the waiter obeyed him instantly. How come?

"And why did he empty my suitcase? We didn't pay the kind of money that entitles us to the services of a personal valet. I'm thinking our crew has a friend on the police force."

"Of course," Piper cried. "You can always count on a small percentage of the law being corrupt. Signore Moretti is probably in on it with them. Scamming wealthy tourists is a great way to make extra money on the side."

"Absolutely," Olivia exclaimed. "When we told him the Duchess of Kingston was making the reservation, he probably alerted the others who told that pompous security guard to check us out when we went through customs at the airport."

Piper nodded. "The moment he saw we were wearing the Duchesse pendants, he informed his cohorts. They figured there was a lot more where that came from and scrambled to get the boat ready."

"A chef who looks like him cooking for royalty—I don't believe that for a minute!" Olivia raged.

Greer moaned. "When I think I told you to ask if we could have the boat exclusively if we paid them another $1,000 apiece!"

Olivia shook her head. "They must have rubbed their hands with glee."

"Well they're not going to get away with it!" Piper declared. "When we reach Genoa we'll go straight to the American Consulate and tell them what's happened."

"You mean *if* we reach Genoa." Greer had been looking out the porthole. "Take a look, guys. We're still going east, not west."

"Why aren't we surprised?"

The three of them stared at each other before Olivia said, "We'll swim for it as soon as we get close enough to land or the nearest passing boat. Which ever comes first."

Piper's eyes rounded. "You know we could?"

"Of course we could. There's no current here as strong as the one in the Hudson. If we wear some casual skirts and tops instead of bathing suits when we go up on deck, they won't suspect anything," Olivia reasoned. "Especially if we keep on our sandals."

"Good idea," Greer said. "And we should all keep together so it looks like I'll have to use clothes from one of your cases."

"That's fine. What about our passports and tickets?"

Greer had been thinking about that. "Leave them. We'll line our bras with the twenty-dollar bills we brought with us. When we reach shore and tell the police what happened, our abductors will be hauled in and we'll recover our stuff.

"But just in case something happens and we don't get our belongings or pendants back, I'll tuck mine inside my bra so we'll have at least one heirloom left for posterity."

"Good thinking, Greer." Olivia walked over to the baskets. ''Better eat some more fruit and chocolate to give us energy, guys. We're going to need it.''

In twenty minutes they were fed, dressed and had worked out their strategy.

''Everybody ready with a life jacket?'' Greer whispered. They didn't plan to use them, but would take them topside so it looked like they were following the rules.

Her sisters nodded.

''Then let's go. Play it cool.''

They couldn't have asked for a more calm, blue sea. Enough of a breeze filled the sails for the boat to move without the help of the engines. Conditions were perfect to escape.

Once they dived overboard, the crew would have to take down the sails before starting up the engines to catch them. The girls planned to grab that window of opportunity to swim beyond their reach.

All three of their captors were on deck. The first mate stood next to the man named Luc who lounged against the cockpit's exterior where his cane rested. No doubt they were both talking to the captain, relishing thoughts of the night ahead.

Greer turned her head in the other direction to smirk. Relish away all you want. It won't do you any good.

Following Olivia's lead, she and Piper purposely worked their way to the bow. To her joy the boat appeared to be making for a headland. Another fifteen minutes in the same direction and the girls would have no problem swimming the rest of the distance.

Using their life jackets for pillows, they stretched out to enjoy the sun. Though it was after seven o'clock, the rays still felt warm against their skin.

No sooner had Greer closed her eyes than she sensed the shark's presence. A shark that could hunker down next to her. A shark that smelled of the soap's tang he'd used in the shower.

"What a tragedy you didn't stay in the dining room long enough to enjoy the rack of lamb entré Luc prepared."

She sucked in her breath. "We can't eat fish, and didn't realize he'd prepared anything else. I'm sure it made a tasty meal for you," Greer murmured without opening her eyes.

"His cooking is always a treat. You disappointed him by not eating it. At the moment he's very fragile."

What tripe was the first mate feeding her now? "Why is that?"

"He was in a terrible accident and is lucky to still have both legs. In spite of his pain, he prepared a culinary masterpiece for you. The least you could do tonight before going to bed is ask one of your sisters to thank him for his trouble."

You mean you want Piper or Olivia to join him in his bed and give him comfort. Good grief! The man was transparent. Talk about a ship of fools!

"Are you saying he's one of those chefs who's known to get volatile when he thinks he's been slighted?"

"That's the wrong choice of word, Greer. You and your sisters hurt him with their comments just now. Do you want that on your conscience, too?"

"Too—" she blurted.

"*Si, bellissima.* Your lips are to die for, but you stab me repeatedly in the heart with your rapier tongue."

Greer didn't know whether to laugh or cry. One minute he frightened her with his overpowering male charisma…the next minute he turned on an irresistible charm that reduced her bones to jelly.

She couldn't keep up with him, and would probably have forgiven him anything if she hadn't found out he was a thief.

"If that's all you came over here to tell me, then I'd prefer to sunbathe alone."

"We're hardly alone, Greer, and with all those clothes on, there's little of you exposed. Fortunately for me I have memories of last night when I saw much more of the flawless skin you're wise to keep covered. Those images will keep the fire burning hot until tomorrow."

An involuntary tremor rocked her body. "Tomorrow?"

"Um. The secret blue grotto I was telling you about is just outside San Remo, the next stop on your itinerary."

"But you're not following our itinerary."

She peeped at him to see his reaction. For a split second she thought she glimpsed the blaze of raw desire in his eyes before his lids lowered like a shutter against a window.

"Until the Grand Prix is over, you will have difficulty avoiding the wall-to-wall bodies as you try to wade ashore at Monterosso. In fact with so many tourists, it will be impossible to see the Riviera di Levante and do it justice.

"Since you seem to have a particular liking for Dumas, I thought tonight you might like to visit the Villa dei Mulini, Napoleon's retreat while he was in exile on the island of Elba."

Elba.

Just the word conjured up a bygone age of history and enchantment she'd only read about in books.

Was he hoping the mention of Napoloen would cause her to divulge more information about her royal Italian heritage so he could find out if there were other pieces of jewelry for the taking?

"If you like, we'll snorkel at nearby Isola Pianosa in the morning. Its sea bed lies in a preserved park no one can enter without advance permission. In my opinion it is one of the most beautiful underwater sights in the world."

Which underwater sight was he really talking about?

The one where he coaxed her into swimming au naturel with him? And afterward they would make wild, primitive love on some deserted beach beneath a hot sun?

Yes, she could imagine it all, in full Technicolor. If he weren't a scoundrel, she had a feeling he could talk her into doing just about anything...

"After you've enjoyed brunch," he went on chatting her up, "we'll stop at Monte Cristo Island and look for buried treasure. Who knows what we'll find?" he drawled in that seductive way that could only mean one thing to a predator like him. It sent a voluptuous shiver though her body.

"I know exactly what we'll find, *signore*. I did my homework before we came to Italy. It's nothing but a pile of desolate rocks that I have no desire to see. I prefer the humanity at Monterosso."

"Inebriated humanity," he came back quietly. "Tourists who have no idea they're lying on a battlefield where an ancient Roman family fought against the invaders from Pisa. But if that is your wish..."

"It is." On that note she turned on her side away from him.

Greer couldn't believe it when she felt his lips against the smooth stem of her neck. She swallowed hard and stared anywhere except at him. He didn't know the meaning of the word fair. The man had refined the art of going for the jugular.

If she continued to resist him, she wouldn't put it past him or his lusty band of thieves to haul them off the boat to the castle and lock them inside while they made their getaway with the loot.

Not only would it be a much needed balm to their dented male egos, it would satisfy their idea of poetic justice for three upstart Americans who'd given them such a hard time.

Except for one brief moment of insanity when Greer had known rapture in his arms.

I have news for you, Max or whatever your real name is. You haven't seen anything yet!

After a minute she lifted her head to meet her sisters' glances. By the expression on their faces, they'd decided the town of Lerici, or whatever, was close enough to reach. Max had started to make his way back to his cousins; now was the time to carry out their plan.

Olivia gave the thumbs-up signal.

"All for one, one for all," Piper whispered.

In a great lunge they bounded over the railing into the warm, blue water. Together they cleaved the gentle waves with swim-meet speed toward the shore.

Max entered the cockpit with a grimace. Nic flashed him a questioning glance. "What's wrong now?"

"Contact the harbor police and tell them to have a cruiser waiting at the dock. Since nothing I've said or done has broken Greer down enough to give me information, perhaps the threat of the law will put the fear in her. I'm through playing games with the *signorine*. I want to know how they got those pendants," he bit out moodily.

Nic had already started phoning when Max turned to Luc. "Keep a close eye on our precious cargo while I go below to find Greer's pendant. Left unattended, I wouldn't put it past our resourceful guests to grab the kayaks and take off."

Luc frowned. "You think they'd go that far in order to get back to Monterosso?"

"Further." Max chewed on the underside of his lip for a minute. "When was the last time you saw a stone cold sober female wearing the Duchesse pendant plunge head-first into the pool of the Splendido with all her clothes on?"

A gruntlike sound came out of Luc. "Point taken."

After Signorina Greer's surprising display of passion in his arms a little while ago, Max had assumed he had her exactly where he wanted her. But it appeared he was mistaken. The enticing little vamp with the amethyst eyes had been playacting the whole time.

Filled with a negative surge of adrenaline because her performance was one he would never forget, Max left the cockpit first. His gaze flitted automatically to the bow before he stopped dead in his tracks. All he could see were three life jackets lying exactly where the women had left them.

Luc saw what Max saw and moved fast for a man with a cane. "The kayaks are still there. The women must have gone below for something. I'll check."

Perhaps Luc was right, but Max had already learned that the enigmatic Duchess triplets played the game of life by a totally different set of rules.

Following his gut instinct which was telling him something didn't feel right, he retraced his steps to the cockpit where Nic was still on the phone. He grabbed the binoculars, stepped back outside and lifted them to his eyes.

Sure enough about a third of the distance from the boat to the shore he saw three heads of gold bobbing up and down in the water. They swam like a school of well trained dolphins. Surprise grabbed him by the throat to witness such a stunning sight.

He moved inside the cockpit once more. "Our guests have jumped overboard without their life jackets."

*"Madre de Dios!"*

"Your concern is wasted on them. They can swim like fish and will reach the shore before long. Tell the police to draw alongside and pull them out pronto!"

Another minute and Luc appeared with three passports and airline tickets in hand. "You were right, Max. I should never have underestimated them. Take a look at this!'' He opened Greer's jewelry case. It was empty.

As pure revelation poured through Max, his mouth thinned to a white line of anger.

"No one leaves a passport behind. Not unless they have an 'in' with someone high up in diplomatic circles who can help them.''

Nic's gaze locked with his. ''That would have to be our jewel thief. Someone operating in our family's inner circle as a friend who happens to own a police commissioner or two?''

"Fausto Galli.''

"Why not? He was the one who called you in London to tell you three women had been detained at the airport wearing identical pendants.''

''Such irresistible bait in more ways than one,'' Luc murmured.

Max sucked in his breath. There was little point in responding to Luc's comment when it was a fact that needed no embellishment.

"That was their purpose, of course,'' Nic concluded. ''The whole thing has been a setup from the moment they made a reservation with Fabio.''

''You're right. Their escape from the bow was no accident, either. Those women are powerful swimmers. I have no doubt they left the boat to meet a prearranged contact at Monterosso in order to hand over the pendant. Most likely someone handpicked by Galli.''

Luc nodded. ''It makes perfect sense. The jewel thief plants the original and two fake pendants on the women to confuse everyone. Then he puts you on their trail so *you* will eventually catch them and put them behind bars.

''Everyone will be happy and think the case is closed. You'll have your pendant back, Signore Galli will find a way to get the Americans' sentences reduced for good behavior, and in the meantime—''

''And in the meantime the real culprit keeps the rest of the family's collection and is free to go on stealing more jewels without fear of suspicion,'' Max finished for him. ''Your reasoning makes an incredible amount of sense.

''Luc? Help me with the sails while Nic starts up the engines. On our way to the dock, I'll make a call to Signore Galli and tell him that since the theft took place in Colorno, the situation is longer in his jurisdiction.''

''He's not going to like that,'' Nic warned.

''But there won't be a thing in hell he can do about it. Especially when I inform him I've instructed the police commissioner in Emilia-Romagna to make arrangements for the Americans *and* the pendant to be transferred from the police boat to the jail in Colorno.''

''Better tell the commissioner to split up the triplets so they can't plan another escape. Their minds think alike which makes them particularly dangerous.''

''I'm way ahead of you, Luc.''

Max's eyes glittered as he studied his two cousins. ''Let the Duchesses of Kingston get a taste of life in an Italian prison. It will give them an education they've been needing. Then we'll deal with them in our own time, on our turf and in our own way. *Capisce?*''

Several deep chuckles ensued.

''Sooner…or later,'' he drawled, ''I'll come up with a plea bargain they'll have to accept. We'll be able to flush out the thief masquerading as our family friend, and that will be the end of it.''

# CHAPTER SIX

GREER looked through the bars of the cell at the overweight prison guard. The commissioner in the main office had put him in charge of her.

"Is everyone around here crazy? The police were supposed to arrest those wretched jewel thieves out on that catamaran. Instead they arrested my sisters and *me*."

"That is not my problem, *signorina*."

Her hands formed fists. "In the United States every person arrested is allowed to make a phone call to their attorney. If you won't let me use a phone, then *you* phone him for me. I left Mr. Carlson's number with the commissioner. I'll pay for it."

Her four, twenty-dollar bills were sopping wet along with her clothes, but they were still considered legal tender.

"Everything in time, *signorina*. It's midnight and no business can be conducted before morning."

"I want to see my sisters."

"That is not possible. Perhaps tomorrow."

"I'd like to know where we are."

"All in good time."

"I demand to know why you're keeping us here!"

"You women are always demanding something, as if this is a luxury hotel instead of a jail. The Duchesse pendant missing since last year was found around your neck. That should answer your question."

Last year? "You mean there's another one?"

"As if you didn't know, *signorina*."

"But I didn't! *We* didn't!" No wonder they were in trouble… "Listen—the one I was wearing was *mine!*"

"How did it come to be in your possession? Can you answer me that? Did it walk out of the museum at the Ducal palace on its own?"

"I'm trying to explain, and you're being very rude, *signore.*"

"You were very rude to steal it."

"How could I steal it when it was given to me by my parents?"

"And the Vatican City was given to me by mine."

"Go ahead and be as nasty as you want. I've told you the truth."

"So your *parents* stole it, is that what you're saying? The House of Parma-Bourbon will be very interested to learn that piece of information."

"That's *not* what I'm saying. It was handed down in the Duchesse family from generation to generation until it was given to my father by his father!"

He threw back his balding head and laughed. "There is no Duchesse family, *signorina.*"

"If you'll look at my passport, you'll see my last name is Duchess, spelled the American way."

"What passport? When the police pulled you out of the sea you did not have one on you."

"We left them on the boat with our airline tickets because we expected to have them returned when the police caught the real jewel thieves!"

"You Americans love a joke." He seemed to find everything she said hilarious and started down the dimly lit hallway.

"Wait! Come back! Please!"

*"Buona notte, signorina."*

She heard a clank.

It was going to be a long night, and a damp one. The

police had supplied them a blanket which she still had wrapped around her. There was another one plus a sheet on the cot against the wall of the miniscule cell. No pillow. In the corner stood an old chamber pot.

Greer couldn't believe it. If all the people arrested had to spend a night in a place like this, they'd probably think twice about ever committing a crime again.

The stuffy cell wasn't cold or hot. Still, she felt so uncomfortable in her damp things, she decided to take everything off and wrap the sheet around her. Hopefully by morning her clothes would be dry.

Her poor leather sandals were ruined, but she wouldn't complain. Not after the sign she once saw at the shoe repair which said, "I felt sorry for the man who had no shoes, until I saw a man who had no feet."

She had to be losing her mind to think about that at a time like this.

There was no place to hang anything, so she spread everything out on the cement floor including the damp blanket. After separating the money so it would dry out too, she lay down on the cot.

The lumpy mattress had to be made out of straw, but she was so exhausted it didn't matter. She stretched out on her side using her arm for a pillow. Catching hold of the other blanket, she drew it over her head. No telling what crawly creatures she'd be spending the night with.

Missing her sisters horribly, she knocked on the wall the way she knocked on the front door at home to let them know she was there.

If one of them was lying on a cot on the other side of it, maybe they would hear her and answer back. But after five minutes of bruising her knuckles against the rough plaster, she gave up and closed her eyes.

Their plan to escape had gone without a flaw. It had seemed like destiny when the police cruiser came alongside them and the authorities offered to help them aboard. But then fate played a cruel joke. What happened next she didn't want to think about.

After handing them a blanket, the police took them to the dock, then hauled them into a van without any windows and no explanation. They must have been on the road several hours, only to be dumped here, her pendant confiscated.

What a laugh Max must have had as he and his cohorts sailed away scot-free, possessors of two pendants, one of which might be the authentic piece.

Sorry, Daddy. You and Mother should never have left us money to "try" to find a husband. We're no good in that department.

The men who want to marry us, we don't want.

And the men we shouldn't want...

The memory of a certain male mouth closing over hers took her breath. She pressed her sore knuckles against her lips, wishing she could drive away the ache that had never left her body since he'd first kissed her.

"Signore di Varano! This is a great pleasure."

"Commissioner? Allow me to introduce my cousins, Lucien de Falcon and Nicolas de Pastrana. We're here to interrogate the prisoners."

"What a tragedy that sisters so beautiful have found themselves on the wrong side of the law."

Max didn't want to hear it. "Did you arrange their cells the way I instructed?"

"Yes. Of course."

"How long have they been here?"

"Approximately two hours."

"Good. Have they caused any problems?"

"Problems? No. The one with the violet eyes was dismayed to be shut up without knowing her crime. I must admit I was moved."

Despite his frustration over their incredible disappearing act, Max had to struggle not to laugh. "Did you enlighten her?"

"*Si.*"

"How did she respond?"

"She protested her innocence. At that point they *all* protested their innocence and demanded to phone their attorney long distance. The one with the aqua eyes put a damp twenty dollar bill across my palm for a bribe."

A sound bordering on a chuckle broke from Nic.

"The one with the flame-blue eyes informed me every prisoner in the United States is given a square meal their first night in jail and she was in need of one. It was very amusing as she clearly expected me to comply with her wishes. She, too, handed me a damp twenty-dollar bill."

"Mademoiselle Olivier had her chance to eat earlier," Luc declared in a cold tone, but Max noticed his cousin's lips twitching.

The commissioner glanced at the three of them. "All in all, the *signorine* were well behaved. I have to admit I was surprised. They didn't complain about not having a change of clothes or any makeup."

Women that beautiful didn't need makeup, but Max said something quite different to the commissioner. "That's because these sisters happen to be professional thieves."

"They must be to have carried off the jewelry collection without being detected. Per your instructions I ordered the guards to take them to different floors for the night where they've been put in isolation."

"Excellent. May I have the pendant please."

"Of course." The commissioner opened the drawer of his desk. The police had put it in a bag they used for forensic evidence. He handed it to Max who put it in the pocket of his jeans.

Now that he possessed all three, he would have them examined by Signore Rossi who would know immediately which one was the genuine article.

"If you'll inform the guards we're ready to begin our questioning of the prisoners." Three foreign beauties, alike in some ways, different in others. Intelligent, unpredictable. And all of them...criminals.

The commissioner nodded and picked up his phone to summon them. No longer smiling, Max told his cousins he'd meet up with them in an hour before they returned to the villa. The balding guard beckoned him down a hallway and through a door that had to be unlocked.

"She's in the middle cell of that corridor where there aren't any other prisoners."

"Did she tell you anything you felt could be important?"

"Only that her parents gave her the pendant she was wearing, thereby admitting that they must have stolen it. Of course she said it had been passed down from generation to generation in the Duchesse family. I told her there was no such family."

"I see. Thank you for the information. I'll knock when I'm ready to leave."

"*Bene.*"

In the shadowy light, the first thing Max noticed were her sandals set out to dry. Next to them lay her skirt, her top, then her underwear. His eyes traveled over each item neatly placed in a row down to the individual twenty-dollar bills. Four of them to be exact.

He was intrigued by the way her mind worked. How orderly she was. There was something essentially feminine about the arrangement. Very prim and proper, yet oddly forlorn because it represented all her worldly possessions.

When his gaze discovered her body cocooned in a

prison blanket and huddled against the cell wall on the narrow, insubstantial cot, he experienced a strange tightness in his chest.

But the possibility that she'd heard voices when the guard opened the outer door and she was only pretending to sleep, hardened his resolve to vet her.

"*Signorina?* Come! Wake up!" He rapped on the bars.

She stirred and rolled toward him, still covered in the blanket. "Are you going to let me make my phone call now?" By the sound of her voice, she was still half-asleep.

"To whom?"

"Walter Carlson."

"Who is he?"

"My father's attorney."

"Why not phone your father?"

"I can't, he's dead."

Max blinked. His experience in the courtroom questioning hostile witnesses led him to believe she was telling the truth.

"Where does this attorney live?"

"In Kingston, New York. He'll vouch for my sisters and me."

"He'll have to do a lot more than that, *signorina.* You've passed yourself off as a relative of the House of Parma-Bourbon, and you're in possession of the stolen Duchesse pendant. All of which constitutes a major crime against the Duchy of Parma. I'm afraid you're facing a stiff prison term."

Greer had heard that distinctive male voice before. Her eyelids fluttered open. She sat up so fast, the blanket slipped to the floor.

In the semidarkness she could see the first mate's powerful physique standing in the hall outside her cell. More, she could feel those eyes of black flame scrutinizing her, scorching whatever part of her skin the sheet didn't cover.

With her heart tripping all over the place, she clutched the scratchy material to her neck. "You have your nerve coming here when *you're* the one who should be behind bars, *signore.*"

"I'm afraid I wasn't the one caught wearing the pendant around my neck when the police plucked you and your sisters from the sea."

"But you stole the other two pendants, so don't bother denying it!"

"I had no intention of doing so."

The man was amoral.

"How did you get in here? No—don't bother to answer that question. You're all so corrupt there's no point."

"All?" His demand came out sounding like ripping silk.

"What part of that word don't you understand? *All*," she repeated. "Every last one of you down to the captain, the chef, the owner of the boat, the commissioner, the guard, the waiter at the Splendido. Need I go on?

"You're all members of that good old boy network. You scratch my back. I'll scratch yours. It's sickening."

His fingers curled around the bars as if he'd like to get them around her neck. "Since I saw pretty good evidence of the good old girl network in operation today when you executed your escape from the *Piccione*, that's a lot like the pot calling the kettle black, wouldn't you say?"

Her chin lifted a little higher. "I'd say your knowledge of American sayings makes you out to be an even more worldly con artist thief than I'd first supposed.

"But the last laugh's going to be on you when you try to sell off those pendants and discover they're not worth more than a couple of hundred American dollars a piece."

"And what about the one you were wearing when you swam for it?" he reminded her. "Are you going to tell me it's only worth two hundred American dollars, too?"

"What if I am?"

"No jury on earth will believe it. Not when you chose to leave your passport behind, something not even silver and gold can buy if you should happen to end up in the wrong country."

"This is the wrong country all right. Nevertheless, a passport *can* be replaced, *signore.* A family heirloom can't..." Her voice trailed off.

"Ah—now we're getting somewhere."

"Getting somewhere? You're sounding more and more like a slick-tongued lawyer with every word. Why don't you pick on a real criminal, like the one the guard said stole a pendant from the museum?"

"Don't think we haven't tried," he admitted with breathtaking honesty.

"You know something? Though you'll probably continue to get away with your perfidy in this life, you won't in the next!"

"Then I guess we'll burn together, *signorina.* If you recall we were already halfway consumed by the flames in your stateroom today."

She swallowed hard. "Only a real playboy would remind me."

"There speaks a woman who instead of slapping my face enjoyed every breathtaking moment of it. If your sisters hadn't chosen that moment to interrupt us..."

"Yes?" Greer prodded. "Would you have made an honest woman of me and asked me to *marry* you?"

After a pregnant silence, she heard a sharp intake of breath. "Is *that* what this has been all about? *Marriage?*"

A smile of satisfaction broke out on her face. "For such a clever jewel thief, I'm surprised it has taken you this long to figure it out."

\*     \*     \*

Max was surprised, too. Stunned was more like it. He'd wanted a confession, so why all of a sudden didn't it sit well with him?

He and his cousins had been forced to deal with fortune hunters all their adult lives. So far they'd been able to spot them and take the necessary steps to elude them. It was the unpleasant if not ugly part that went with the territory of belonging to the House of Parma-Bourbon.

"So...the whole pendant business was a ruse to win an introduction that could result in a marriage proposal?"

"Exactly. But I suppose it's poetic justice that the men we targeted turned out to be several degrees more unscrupulous than ourselves."

Just when he thought he had things figured out, she said something that shot his theories all to hell. "Then you admit the pendants are copies of the original."

"Except for one of them."

"The one your family inherited."

"Yes."

Max cursed softly. This woman had the ability to twist him in knots. "Which one of you was the mastermind behind that plot?" He might as well hear the rest. In truth he'd never in his life been this frustrated and entertained all at the same time.

"Our parents. But only indirectly," she amended.

"*How* indirectly?"

"We could only use the money from the Husband Fund our father willed to us to go spouse hunting."

Husband Fund? Spouse hunting? A bark of laughter escaped his throat. "How much money?"

"Oh, $15,000. $5,000 apiece."

"I thought the pendants were only worth $200."

"They are, except for the real one and I have no idea how much it's worth. Since we're triplets, and there was only one pendant, our parents had two more made up just like it. They gave them to us on our sixteenth birthday for us to pass on to our future children.

"That was the whole point of the Husband Fund, of course. Mom and Dad wanted to ensure there would be another generation of Duchesses. That's something none of us is interested in yet."

Max's eyes closed tightly for a minute. Was this one of those cases where her story had to be true because no one could manufacture such a fantastic tale?

"Anyway, we used the fund for this trip and to charter the *Piccione*."

"Why did you pick the *Piccione*?" This ought to be good.

"Because Daddy always called us his pigeons. You know, in honor of our ancestor the Duchess of Parma who had a pigeon named after her. It's on our business logo."

Just as he'd suspected, whoever had coached these triplets was intimately associated with his family and its history.

"*What*, exactly, is on your logo?"

"The white Duchesse pigeon!"

More and more Max felt he was in the middle of some amazing dream. She seemed to delight in weaving lies. "And this business…what kind did you say it was again?"

"I didn't. We own a company called Duchesse Designs."

Max rubbed bridge of his nose. "What is it you design?"

"Calendars. Actually Piper does the drawings and Olivia does the marketing."

"And what do *you* do?" This was getting better and better.

"I do everything else."

"Like what for instance?"

"Provide the research and keep the books."

"I see."

"I'm surprised you're asking all these questions. If you and your cohorts weren't so obsessed with taking advantage of rich women, you would have noticed our samples in the bottom of Piper's suitcase while you were rummaging through our personal belongings."

He blinked.

"We passed out some to a few distributors in Genoa yesterday hoping to expand our company to an international business."

So much information had been thrown his way, Max could scarcely digest it, let alone decide what part if any of it was true. But he did seem to recall Signore Galli telling him the *signorine* had come to Europe for a little business, as well as pleasure.

The notes made by the police officers assigned to tail the women after they'd left the airport would clear that up in a hurry.

"You still haven't answered my question about why you chose the *Piccione*."

"I've been leading up to that. When we got on the internet and were looking at a list of catamarans to charter because they were cheaper than a yacht, we saw that one of them was called the *Piccione*. It seemed like fate, so we clicked on to it. As it turns out, it was the biggest mistake we ever made!"

"Do not worry, *signorina*. If you cooperate, we might be able to arrive at a bargain which will be mutually advantageous for all."

There was a prolonged silence. "I knew it!" Her voice came out sounding more like a growl. "Admit that one of your cronies on the police force tipped you off that three women wearing the Duchesse pendant would be staying at the Splendido!

"Admit you were up to no good following me and my sisters around! Explain why the waiter obeyed you like a servant!

"Oh yes, and please explain if you can without lightning striking you, how you could suddenly show up on the *Piccione* as the first mate if you hadn't been orchestrating lucrative conspiracies like these for years! Answer me *that!*"

Her challenge brought an effective end to a conversation that had held him spellbound. There were a few dozen matters he needed to research before he spoke to her again.

"All in good time, *signorina.*"

"That's what the guard said. Typical male rhetoric. You don't fool me. You came to the jail to find out if my sisters and I have more jewels hidden away somewhere.

"Well you won't get that information out of me, not even if the commissioner gave you a key to this cell. I'm warning you now, your powers of seduction leave a lot to be desired.

"Any coward can manhandle a woman confined to a life jacket or behind bars. I have to tell you I would have been a lot more impressed and possibly more forthcoming if you'd tried your best technique while you were escorting me back to my room at the Splendido.

"For a Riviera playboy, I have to tell you that on a scale of one to ten, ten being the ultimate male, you came in a four. Unfortunately a four still isn't passing. Even Don rated a five. Sorry."

"Don? As in Don Juan?" he scathed.

"No. Don as in Don Jardine, an American. I should have given him more credit the first time.

"*Arrivederci, Signore Mysterioso.* Oh—before I forget. On your way out to plot your next heist with your henchmen, turn off the hall light, will you? I'd like to get some sleep."

His body stiffened. "I guess you can try to rest, but for a woman who has as much on her conscience as you do, I don't hold out great hope for you. *Ciao, bellissima.*"

His mood foul, Max went in search of his cousins. He found both of them outside the door to the commissioner's office. When they saw him, they stopped pacing.

"You look like the survivor of an explosion," Nic observed.

"I was going to say the same thing about both of you."

A nerve pulsed at the side of Luc's mouth where a tiny scar from the crash was still healing. "You won't believe what I have to tell you. It has to do with that old wives' tale concerning one of Marie-Louise's granddaughters who supposedly had a liaison with a monk.

"Mademoiselle Olivia claims she and her sisters are the descendants of their love child."

Max's jaw went slack. "That rumor was proven false years ago and few people outside the immediate family ever even heard of it. Can there be any doubt our jewel thief is someone operating from the inside? When we wring a full confession from the *signorine,* we won't have to look far to find the culprit."

"The story goes from one *absurdité* to another," Luc declared. "According to our lovely jailbird, the granddaughter was purported to have suffered a miscarriage. In reality she delivered a son whom the monk, her lover, secretly christened with the last name Duchesse to protect his identity.

"He then arranged to have the baby taken to Corsica where it was raised by a childless woman loyal to the Bonapartes. Inside the infant's blankets he'd wrapped the pendant.

"Several generations later that pendant traveled to America where the Duchesse name was changed to

Duchess. It ended up in New York in the hands of the father of the *belles mesdemoiselles.*

"Not wanting to slight his offspring, he had two more pendants made identical to the original so they would each have one to hand down to their posterity."

The sheer scope of the lie left all of them dumbfounded.

Max eventually glanced at Nic. "Did Signorina Piper tell you the same fiction?"

"No—she fed me another lie," Nic said with asperity. "Something crazy about these pigeon drawings she has done for their family calendar business.

"Get this—" he said in a burst of laughter. "They call the female Violetta, after the Duchess. Since this fictitious monk who remained a mystery for over a century had no first name, she and her sisters decided to call him Luigio, a subtle distortion of the second half of Maria-Luigia's name."

A flashback of a certain moment in the pool of the Splendido hit Max squarely in the gut.

*Greer—Your name is as unique as you are. Why don't you guess mine?*

*Luigio?*

The whole time Max had been toying with her, she'd been playing him for a complete fool!

"She says that one of her great-grandfathers, Alberto Duchess, served in World War I in the Signal Corps. Are you ready for this?" Nic's eyes appeared dazed as they traveled from Luc to Max. "He raised Duchesse pigeons for a hobby.

"One of them carried a message that saved the lives of several hundred men and received a medal of honor from Great Britain. Señorita Piper says the medal is at home among their family mementos."

Max's dark head reared back. "Signorina Greer told me

to look in her sister's suitcase and I would find samples of this calendar.''

''Their luggage is in the car,'' Nic declared. ''Do you think the samples are really there?''

No one said anything or made a move to walk outside. Max suspected his cousins were holding back for the same reason he was. But they couldn't stand there forever smoldering with curiosity. It was four in the morning and they were dead on their feet.

Letting out a curse he finally said, ''Come on. Let's find out and get this over with.''

They made their way to the restricted parking area. Luc trailed because at this point he was favoring his cane. They were the only people moving about in the dark.

Max opened the trunk of the estate car they'd driven over from the villa. The inside light made it possible to see enough without needing a flashlight. Nic found the case with the initials PD on it and opened the locks.

After feeling around her clothes, he produced a large square manila envelope. As his cousin proceeded to empty the contents, Max found himself holding his breath.

Out came six calendars.

Luc reached for one of them. ''Men's Most Notable Quotes About Women,'' he read aloud.

''For Women Only,'' Nic mouthed the title of another sample. Max grabbed for a similar calendar and opened the cover to January's quote for the month.

*So Many Men... So Few Who Can Afford Me.*

Sure enough, *there* was the female pigeon Violetta, dressed in a gown and jewels. The male, Luigio, looking weary and dejected, tagged behind.

Max's eyes widened to realize they'd entered an exclusive designer shop on one of the fashionable boulevards in *Parma*. Next to a pair of shoes, a handbag and dress she'd drawn placards showing astronomical prices both in lire and dollars.

Astonished, he turned to February's quote.

*Coffee, Chocolate... Men. Some Things Are Just Better Rich.*

This time the two pigeons sat in an elegant pastry shop near the Teatro Farnese in Parma drinking espresso and munching on their world famous chocolate biscotti. While Luigio looked longingly at her, Violetta played footsie beneath the table with a well-dressed Italian pigeon wearing the ducale corona emblem. *Incredible.*

March's quote.

*Don't Treat Me Any Differently Than You Would The Queen.*

It was yet another drawing of poor, helpless, love-smitten Luigio throwing down his cloak for the treacherous yet delectable Violetta who was visiting Langhirano where you could see the very long, narrow windows, shuttered and open—designated to ventilate the aging hams.

April's quote.

*Behind Every Successful Woman Is A Woman.*

His curiosity insatiable by now, Max studied each rendition with total absorption. He came to November.

*Ginger Rogers Did Everything Fred Astaire Did, But She Did It Backward And In High Heels.*

There was Luigio in a tux and top hat. Violetta wore a gown and high heels while she danced backward on the staircase of the Palazzo della Pilotta in Parma.

Like being mesmerized at the scene of a fire where you couldn't look away, he turned to December.

*A Man's Gotta Do What A Man's Gotta Do. A Woman's Got To Do What He Can't.*

The irony of the quote twisted something unpleasant in his gut. Finally he took in the sketch of the enormously pregnant Violetta lying on a gurney in the Torrile Bird Hospital in Parma while Luigio lay passed out on the floor.

Not that many of his own countrymen knew about the bird refuge his family helped fund. Max was convinced Signorina Greer's research had to be aided and abetted by someone on the inside.

He also had to admit the two pigeons exuded so much individual human charm and personality, one could only marvel. This clever, stunning creation based on bits of myth and reality would have universal appeal for women, even for those ignorant of Parma or its history.

But the acerbic quotes he could imagine coming out of Greer's succulent mouth, served with a contemporary sting, which he as a man felt like the lash of a whip, had wiped the smile off his face.

"Look on the back." Luc's grating voice broke the unnatural stillness. No doubt he and Nic were still smarting from the quotes, too.

Max turned his calendar over. At the bottom center was an oval with a stylized Duchesse Pigeon and the words Duchesse Designs printed inside the rim.

"The existence of the calendars doesn't mean they're innocent of the crime," Luc proclaimed in a wooden voice. "A good liar always mixes in enough truth to be convincing."

Nic exhaled sharply. "You're right."

By tacit agreement they put the calendars back in the suitcase. Max shut the trunk before getting in the car to head for the villa. "As soon as Signore Rossi arrives at his office later on this morning, we'll show him the pendants. When we learn the truth about them, then we'll know what to do with the *signorine*."

# CHAPTER SEVEN

ITALY'S top jewelry authenticator of their national treasures barely glanced at the first two pendants front and
back before declaring them fakes. But the moment he
picked up the third one, he got excited.

Max exchanged speculative glances with Nic and Luc
before they followed Signore Rossi to his worktable where
he placed the pendant under a special light. With his loupe
he wore like a pair of glasses, he performed a meticulous
examination.

His finger tapped on it. "Yes," he said after several
minutes, nodding his gray head. "This piece has Tocelli's
mark in the space between the intertwining D and P on
the back. *Momento*—" He reached for his workbook con-
taining photocopies and drawings of the Maria-Luigia collection.

Max's body grew more rigid as he watched Signore
Rossi turn to the section on the Duchesse pendant for final
verification.

The news that the original had indeed surfaced again
meant the theory he and his cousins had come up with still
held; Signorina Greer and her sisters were part of a bigger
conspiracy.

Which also meant that except for the calendars, everything else Max had heard pour forth from her provocative
lips in that jail cell was pure spin!

For some reason he couldn't fathom, he had to admit he
was disappointed. When he stole a glance at his cousins,
their sobriety revealed a startling bleakness that probably
mirrored his own dark thoughts.

The ticking of an antique clock added a dirgelike quality to the unearthly quiet. Then Max heard a strange cry come out of Signore Rossi who started to grow animated. He removed his glasses and rose to his feet, staring at them as if he'd just seen a vision.

"How did you say you came by this pendant?"

"We recovered it from some Americans who were each wearing one when they flew into Genoa-Sestri airport two days ago."

"Then this means the court artisan who was commissioned to fashion the first pendant, secretly made a second one."

Max's thoughts reeled. He exchanged shocked glances with his cousins before addressing Signore Rossi. "With all due respect, you must be mistaken."

"No!" The old man shook his head emphatically. "This is the original pendant. There can be no mistake. But it's not the same original that was stolen with the collection from the museum. The Tocelli mark is there, but more elongated. Come. See for yourselves."

In a matter of minutes Max and his cousins had witnessed irrefutable proof that two authentic pendants *did* exist. As they eyed each other in wonder, all sorts of new possibilities flooded his mind.

If the *signorine* had nothing to do with the theft, then it stood to reason they'd been telling the truth about everything else. Furthermore, with the possession of another original pendant, it could be used to flush out the real thief.

"This is great cause for celebration," Signore Rossi exclaimed, oblivious to their reaction.

"It's fantastic news, *signore,* but you must say nothing about it," Nic cautioned in a grave tone before Max could. "Not until the person who stole the collection is apprehended and the other pendant returned. Then both can be displayed to the public."

"We're certain someone with close ties to our family was behind the theft," Max explained. "With this pendant, we might be able to lay a trap for them, I'm sure they would want this one, too, but we'll need your full cooperation."

Signore Rossi nodded. "Of course. Of course. What can I do to help?"

Luc's eyes had grown hooded. "No one outside this room must know what we've discovered until we're ready to have it announced. That means you can't say anything to anyone. Is that clear?"

"*Si.*"

Max looked around. "Do you have something I can put the pendants in for safe keeping?"

"Right here." He pulled several velvet pouches out of one of the drawers.

In an economy of movement Max put the original in one, the other two in the second little bag. Once he'd closed the drawstrings and the pouches were put safely away in his pockets, he took hold of the old man's hands and shook them.

"One day soon we'll put the real jewel thief behind bars. When that happens, you'll know the extent of our gratitude for your help and cooperation."

After saying goodbye, no one spoke again until they'd gone out to the car where Max eyed his cousins. "Before either of you says a word, let me tell you about the Husband Fund."

"The *what?*" Luc's expression was comical.

"To quote Signorina Greer, it's a fund for husband hunting."

Nic shook his head. "Husband hunting?"

Judging by their reactions, the subject hadn't come up during their interrogation of the prisoners.

"Of course it might be one of her colossal lies, but after

looking at those calendars, I'm not so sure." His brows lifted. "Do you two want to have a little fun before we get back to more serious family business?"

While Greer was playing a game in her head to keep herself from going crazy, a different guard came down the hall.

"*Buon giorno, signorina.* Did you enjoy your lunch?"

"It was the best toothbreaking roll I ever tried to bite into. I can't wait to see what you're serving for dinner."

"That won't be for a long time." He opened her cell. "The commissioner will see you now."

"How lovely of him."

She followed the guard through the door at the end of the hall and around the corner to the commissioner's office. He stood up as soon as he saw her.

"Sit down, *signorina.* Make yourself comfortable."

"I've been sitting on my cot for over—" She glanced at the clock. "Sixteen hours now, and would rather stand, thank you."

"As you wish." He made that typical Italian gesture with his hands, palms up. It reminded her of someone else she knew. Someone she never wanted to see or think about again.

"I demand to be able to make one phone call to my attorney."

"That won't be necessary. It turns out the pendant your sister was wearing was a copy of the missing Duchesse pendant. I'm sorry you were incarcerated by mistake.

"The first mate of the *Piccione* has been very worried about you and has stayed in constant contact. As soon as I told him you'd been cleared of all charges, your sisters were released into the hands of the crew."

*Nooooooooooo.* For all she knew Olivia and Piper had been kidnapped. She was still entirely convinced the crew were jewelry thieves who didn't believe the girls had no money. They needed help fast.

"He is waiting outside, ready to drive you to the dock at Lerici so you can continue on with your holiday."

Her body froze. No way.

"I would like to use your phone please. I have money."

"As long as it's a local call, be my guest."

So *that* was how he was going to play it. "May I see your phone directory then."

*"If you need a taxi, allow me to take you wherever it is you wish to go, Signorina Greer."* The deep, familiar male voice speaking in heavily accented English came from behind her.

Her back stiffened in response. "No, thanks." She was still facing the commissioner. "The phone directory please, *signore*."

"But I insist," her enemy taunted her.

After no sleep, a crust of week old bread, a thimble of water and no shower or change of clothes, Greer had run out of patience.

She wheeled around, noticing inconsequently that the black-haired god was fresh shaven and wore a cream shirt with tan pants. The fact that his clothes accentuated his well-defined chest and rock-hard legs only increased her rage.

"I'd rather stay in here, thank you." So saying she marched out of the office and down around the corner of the jail where she spied the guard sitting at his post.

"Will you please open the door so I can go back to my cell?"

He flashed her a patronizing smile. "You've been released, *signorina*."

"I'll pay you to lock me in again." She reached down the neck of her top and pulled out two twenty dollars bills to hand him.

"You Americans—" He threw his head back and laughed.

So far every Italian man she'd met was in cahoots against her. This grinning idiot was as awful as the balding guard from last night.

"If you'll appeal to me nicely," came Max's low, velvety voice over her shoulder, "I'll give you something to prove you can trust me."

How did he do that? How did he make her traitorous body respond like a kitten to cream when she knew one lick would be fatal?

Greer nodded her head in disgust before facing him once more. "Nothing but the return of our pendants, our passports and airline tickets would convince me there's the slightest shred of decency in you. Even then—"

"Yes?" he whispered huskily before pulling things out of the pockets of his pants like passports and airline tickets. Last of all came a little velvet pouch. He handed everything to her. When she looked inside, she counted three pendants.

How clever he was! Give her back their possessions knowing she would never abandon her sisters, knowing they were still helpless. And only *he* knew where they'd been taken by his two cohorts.

"You were saying, *signorina*?"

"I was *saying* that *even then*, it would be an empty gesture because it would mean you'd had the pendants appraised and found out you probably couldn't get more than fifty euros a piece for them."

"Seventy-five on the black market."

The temperature in her cheeks had shot up well over a hundred degrees. "I rest my case."

He cocked his dark head. "I hope that was an olive branch of sorts. Let's agree to agree we all got off to a bad start. You came spouse hunting and were sadly disappointed. My co-workers and I went treasure hunting and came up empty-handed.

"But since Signore Moretti has already paid us our wages from the Husband Fund your parents left you, why don't we start over again. I see no reason why we can't all get along for the next nine days before you have to fly home to Ron, was it?"

It gave her some satisfaction to know she'd dented his ego. Otherwise he wouldn't have deliberately pretended he hadn't heard her say "Don."

"You mean there'll be no hidden agenda," she drawled with heavy sarcasm. "We'll just do whatever comes naturally."

He put a hand over his heart. "You still don't trust me. I'm wounded, *signorina*. At the risk of offending you, if you recall when I asked you to swim with me at the Splendido, you didn't exactly turn me down."

"That's true," she admitted honestly. "However if I had, you wouldn't have taken no for an answer. I saw where your eyes were looking. They erupted like black fires when they recognized the pendant."

"If you'd seen the purple flames in yours while you were watching me walk across the tiles toward you…" His voice throbbed. "I felt like I was being consumed alive. There's nothing more flattering to a man."

"Too bad I had to open the cover of the book and find out you rated a four. I'd thought an eight at least."

"And I'd thought the pendant worth a million. What do you say we bury our disappointments and just be friends for the duration of your trip."

It was a trick.

No women could just be friends with men like the crew of the *Piccione*. But it looked like she would have to go along with him a little longer if she hoped to be reunited with her sisters. Once they were together, they would work out a way to lose the crew and disappear.

"Why not?" She threw out her bluff. "As I've learned in business, you win a few, lose a few."

She started walking back toward the main entrance of the jail. In a long stride he'd caught up to her.

"I don't imagine too many men clamor for your calendars."

Good. He'd rifled through her sister's suitcase. She smiled in spite of her issues with him. "You'd be surprised how many of them buy one to get their revenge on the women who rejected them. Kind of a 'look at yourself in the mirror' dark humor."

He reciprocated with a toe-curling smile of his own. "Has Don sent you one lately?"

Don again. "He doesn't need to. It's his company that prints our products."

"The poor devil gets it on all sides. I'd rate him an eight for hanging in there despite the odds."

"Don't feel too sorry for him. He manages to get his perks," she said as she stepped outside into the hot afternoon sun. It was glorious, liberating, after her windowless prison. "Where's your car?"

He put on his sunglasses. "In the alley around the side of the jail."

There were dozens of funny looking little Italian cars lined up like sardines along both sides of centuries old buildings. He walked over to a well-used blue Fiat with a bike rack. She noticed most of the cars had bike racks. To her surprise he opened the trunk first and pulled out her purse.

"Thank you," she murmured before putting the passports and other things inside. To her relief her wallet, comb and lipstick were still there.

"You're welcome. One thing I've learned about a woman. She doesn't feel dressed without one."

There probably wasn't a man alive who knew more about things like that than he did, but she wisely refrained from commenting.

He helped her into the front seat, then went around to the driver's side. While she combed her seaweed washed hair and put on lipstick to moisten her lips, he somehow, but she didn't know how, managed to get them out of there in one deft maneuver without hitting anything.

They'd only gone two blocks when she saw a gleaming white palace standing out from among the other architectural wonders. Her heart started to pound with excitement.

She may not have been to Italy before, but she'd done enough research to recognize it at once. Piper had drawn two of the calendar pages using the palace and gardens for a backdrop.

"After last night's ordeal, most women would not be smiling. What is going on in your mind, *signorina?*"

"The Colorno ducal palace. It was my ancestor's favorite summer residence. To think I spent the night locked up in a jail within walking distance of it. That'll be a story I'll tell to my children someday."

"You plan to have children, *signorina?*"

"Of course. Don't you? Someday I mean?"

"Not my own. No."

Not his own? Ask a silly question—

"The last thing I would wish to do is destroy a belief you've had since childhood, *signorina.* But when your sister told Luc you were related to the Duchesse of Parma through a granddaughter who had a liaison with a monk, I thought it best you know the truth."

She turned a frowning face toward him. "What truth?"

"There was a rumor many years ago about a granddaughter of Maria-Luigia who fell in love with a monk and bore his child. As it turns out, it was a political lie, spun to discredit her so the arranged marriage to her betrothed in France would not take place.''

"How would you know something like that?''

"Luc is the one who can give you more details. He learns many secrets while he prepares meals for his royal employers. I'm sorry.''

She stared at her hands in her lap. ''It doesn't matter. None of us quite believed it, and Daddy wasn't entirely sure about it. Still, it made for an exciting story.''

"And now you have another reason to dislike me.''

"I don't like or dislike you. You mean nothing to me, *signore*.''

"Can I make this up to you by taking you on a tour through the palace before we return to the *Piccione*? It's quite magnificent.''

"I'm sure it is, but no thank you. I prefer to keep my fairy-tale dreams in tact.''

"So you intend to continue the legacy and hand down your pendant to a daughter someday?''

"Yes. Why not. Only maybe I'll start a new rumor of my own.''

He turned to her. ''What rumor would that be?''

"Maybe the artisan who fashioned the pendant was secretly in love with Marie-Louise. Maybe he fathered a son and gave him the last name Duchesse in honor of the woman he could never have.''

"That's a very romantic story, *signorina*. Of the two, I don't know which I like better.''

His mocking voice was the last straw. She'd been right all along. A shark felt no emotion.

"Here. This will help to sustain you until we arrive at the dock.'' He reached in the back behind Greer's seat and produced a bottle of soda.

Warm orange soda. Ugh. But she'd be a fool to refuse it.

"Thank you."

"I know you Americans prefer ice. I'm sorry. Try one of these with it."

Like magic he'd produced a package of cookies. Chocolate biscotti, just like the kind Piper had drawn in that one calendar picture.

After a swig of pop, she took a bite. "Um. They're good. Better than potato chips. I can't stop with just one."

"Potato chips are one of the two things I like best about your country."

"You've been there?"

"Several times."

Funny to think of him in her part of the world and she never knew it. The trail of broken hearts had to be legion. "What's the other?"

"The long legs on American women. I once saw a movie with Betty Grable. Yours remind me of hers."

Her drink sprayed all over her cotton top.

"Are you all right, *signorina?*"

"Yes, of course. I just swallowed the wrong way."

"Soon we will reach the *Piccione*. There's a washer and dryer on board."

"All the comforts of home."

"That is true. It's my favorite home away from home."

"Where *is* your home?"

"Colorno. My family lives in nearby Parma."

No wonder he'd been able to bribe the commissioner! "Will we be passing through there?"

"Only the outskirts I'm afraid. I must congratulate you on the research you've done on Parma for your calendar business. I recognized every backdrop immediately."

"Piper's a genius."

"I agree, but the drawings would not have come to life

without all the details you unearthed. Genius appears to run in the Duchess family.''

''Thank you,'' she whispered. His compliment warmed her clear through. It shouldn't have, not when he was a thief of jewels...and hearts.

''So does beauty,'' he filled in the silence. ''I've seen you in every condition, yet soaking wet, starving, in prison and exhausted, you are even more appealing, if that is possible.''

What was he after now? All this flattery was so unnecessary now, but she had to admit the things he was saying made it difficult for her to breathe normally.

When he reached down to take a cookie for himself, his hand brushed against her thigh. Greer didn't know if it was intentional or not, but her body reacted as if she'd come in contact with a live wire.

''Luc is preparing a welcome home feast for you and your sisters. I must admit I'm looking forward to it, too. In all the excitement with the police and the hours of waiting for you to be released, none of us took the time to eat.''

Of course not. They were too busy trying to find a buyer for the pendants.

She wouldn't believe any of his malarky until she saw her sister's dear faces back on board the catamaran. Only when she'd discovered for herself they'd survived their hideous night in that ghastly jail, would she be able to take a normal breath.

As one kilometer after another unraveled around hills and bends, a delightful smorgasbord of tiny hamlets, ancient villages and farms filled her vision. If she weren't so worried about her sisters, she could enjoy the fabulous landscape.

''Since dinner is quite a few hours away yet, I thought we'd stop here and satisfy our hunger.''

After coming round a bend in the road, she was surprised to see what looked like an open-air festival of some kind being held in a field. There were all kinds of colorful booths and hundreds of people milling around, talking and eating.

"What's going on?"

"We're at the Fiera de Parma."

"Fiera?"

"*Si*—fairground." He parked the car before trapping her gaze. "You're not only lucky enough to be in the capital of Italy's famous 'food valley' where Prosciutto di Parma ham and Parmigian-Reggiano cheese are celebrated— you've been freed from jail in time to enjoy the International Food Exhibition which is only held every two years. Come with me."

When she remarked on the pungent aroma in the air he told her it was white truffles, a local delicacy. Greer had reached the point of starvation some time ago and didn't need to be urged to join him as they moved about among the crowd sampling the delicious displays.

He fed her everything from emerald green olive oil on chunks of chewy Italian bread sprinkled with cheese, to pale, paper-thin slices of tender parma ham that melted in your mouth.

Every so often he popped a fragrant, fleshy black or green olive in her mouth. As if that weren't enough, he stuffed her with ice cream and more biscotti, giving her the true taste of exquisite Italian cuisine.

Yet more than the food was the excitement of feeling his arm around her waist, his fingers brushing against her mouth, the play of his dark eyes traveling over her face while he waited for her approval of something she'd eaten.

This enigmatic stranger who seduced her with a soft caress, a quick smile, a deep laugh, had created a dangerous state of enchantment for Greer. She rebelled at the injustice of having to return to the car...to painful reality.

Silence reigned as they made their descent to the coast where the shimmering water reflected a cloudless sky. The distinctive multihull of the *Piccione* stood out from the few fishing and rowboats still docked in Lerici's small harbor.

He drove the car into a public area where other cars were parked and got out. Greer grabbed her purse and ran ahead of the man she still didn't trust and never would.

"Piper? Olivia?" Until they answered, she wouldn't put one foot on board.

All she got for her shouting was the captain. He stepped out of the cockpit wearing sunglasses and a broad smile that ought to be fined for being too captivating.

*"Buenos tardes, señorita.* Welcome back. Luc and I brought your sisters home from the jail a few hours ago." Hours? "Señorita Olivo had a headache. They both announced they were going straight to bed and didn't want to be disturbed."

Olivia didn't get headaches.

"Prove it!"

*"Momento,"* the man behind her whispered. "I'll ask them to come up on deck so you'll know they're safe."

"Greer!"

Two blond heads suddenly appeared at the top of the stairs.

# CHAPTER EIGHT

THANK heaven!

Greer leaped on board and hurried toward them. They scuttled below to the stateroom they'd used before. Piper locked the door, then they all hugged.

Olivia took one look at her and said, "You've got stains all over you. What happened in your jail cell?"

"Never mind that. We'll talk later." She held up her purse. "The pendants are in here. Max gave them back along with our passports and tickets. He also fed me royally."

"Luc served us a fabulous lunch after they brought us back to the boat."

"They've been exceptionally nice."

"Yeah...well we all know why don't we. They found out our jewels weren't worth enough to bother with, so now they're ready to enjoy *us* for the rest of the trip."

"I'm sure you're right," Piper muttered.

Olivia nodded. "They figure if they feed us and take care of us, we'll be ripe for the picking after the sun goes down."

Greer stared at both of them. "I say we leave for Genoa right now."

"Amen. Everybody grab a suitcase. Let's get out of here before they cast off!"

Greer was first out the door. She almost bumped into Max who grasped her upper arms in a firm grip.

"Where's the fire?" His black eyes scrutinized her. "I thought you would want to shower and rest after your ordeal in Colorno."

Her proud Duchesse nose lifted in the air. It brought their eyes and lips too close for comfort. "I don't need to rest."

He studied her mouth as if he were considering devouring it. What made it so much worse was that she wanted him to.

"I was just coming to ask your sisters if they're ready for their dessert yet. Luc told me to tell them he has made a special *framboise* tart that will satisfy their sweet tooth."

"What sweet tooth?"

"The one you all share," he said in a husky tone. "There is chocolate on your mouth from your last biscotti as we speak, *bellissima*." He brushed at it with his finger before tasting it. The intimate gesture was a reminder of everything they'd shared at the fair.

Crimson flags spotted her cheeks. "We've indulged ourselves long enough, don't you think?" she said before realizing how that must have sounded to him. "Now we're leaving."

Lines marred his handsome features. "To do what?"

"That's our business. Please move out of our way."

"Not until you tell me where you think are you going."

"Oh, I *know* where we're going."

A condescending smile broke out on his enticing male mouth. Prepared for a knock down drag out, Greer was taken off guard when he unexpectedly took a step back so she could proceed.

The girls followed her down the hall and up the stairs to the top deck, all of them carrying their suitcases.

At a glance she could see Luc untying the ropes. Vibrations ran through her feet and legs, alerting her that the captain had started the engine. Without hesitation she raced up the steps with her luggage and stepped onto the dock. Piper and Olivia joined her with their cases.

The first mate walked toward them with his hands on

his hips. His male beauty combined with his sheer audacity burrowed deeply beneath her skin.

Unable to hold back her anger any longer she cried, "So...you were just going to sail off with us after what you've done? No questions asked?"

His dark gaze pierced through to her insides, making her feel quivery and out of control. She hated that feeling.

"We were going to follow your itinerary to the letter. Our first stop for tonight is Monterosso."

"We were supposed to go there last night, but things turned out differently, so we've changed our minds about continuing with this trip."

"I can see that. May I say one thing. Wherever you wish to go, there won't be another train through Lerici for at least two hours. Even then you probably won't be able to get on. It's possible you could end up having to wait till four in the morning."

"Max is right," Luc spoke up. He and the captain had come to stand on the dock next to their partner in crime. "That would be very dangerous for three beautiful, unattached women. With the Grand Prix on tomorrow, transportation is so bad it will be impossible to find a taxi."

"Every hotel room along the coast has been booked for months, *señoritas*," Nic chimed in. "Tell us your destination and we'll take you there in comfort on the *Piccione* without the waiting and the hassle."

The stranger's gaze was riveted on Greer. "I would like to try to make up for the disappointment I gave you during our talk in the car."

"Which disappointment was that?" she fired. "There have been so many."

"When I told you that you have no Italian blood in you. I realize it destroyed a dream for you."

"Max is right," the captain spoke up. "Your Duchesse name came from the French 'Duchesne.'"

"Really?" Greer broke in heatedly. "So our captain-cum resident etymologist is now a professional genealogist, too?"

His white smile was an affront. "*Si, señorita.* They dropped the 'n' and the final 'e' when they arrived in America."

Luc nodded. "I'm afraid the story about an Italian monk who made love to the granddaughter of Maria-Luigia and gave her a son is pure fabrication. We know the news hurts, *mesdemoiselles.*"

The first mate's eyes never left Greer's. "Do not shoot the messenger, instead tell me how I can take away a little of the sting, *bellissima.*"

Oh, brother.

"Admittedly all six of us are liars," she began without preamble, "but if you're being sincere this time, then give us the keys to your car so we can leave for the airport."

"You're planning to return to the States without enjoying the rest of your trip?" he inserted in a silky voice.

"That's not anyone's concern but ours," she declared. "We'll leave the car in the short-term parking at the Genoa airport. You can pick up your keys at the airline ticket counter."

"Why would you fly away now when we've only just started to get to know each other?"

"I know all I want to know!" By now Greer's eyes were spitting purple sparks at him. "With your good old boy network flourishing in this neck of Italy, *signore,* I've no doubt you'll be able to manage perfectly well without your car for three or four hours."

He tossed off one of those careless masculine shrugs that drew her gaze to his remarkable physique. "Be my guest, Greer. We'll help you to the car."

Before she could countenance it, the three men took

hold of their luggage and started walking toward the parking area beyond the dock.

Her sisters flashed her a private message that said they didn't trust the crew as far as they could throw them. Greer flashed them the same message. This was way too easy. There was definitely something wrong here. She could feel it in her bones.

"They could have pulled the distributor cap while we were in our stateroom," Olivia whispered.

Piper nodded. "I guess we'll find out soon enough if it doesn't start."

"It's probably running on fumes by now," Greer theorized. "I wouldn't put it past him to have tampered with the gauge so we'd never be able to tell until it was too late."

"Or—" Olivia rolled her eyes "—the tires will all go flat the minute we try to reach the highway."

"Then we'll drive on the rims as far as we can," Piper stated firmly. "Olivia, you're the designated driver. I'll help navigate."

"I'll sit in the back and be quiet," Greer volunteered.

By the time they reached the Fiat, the men had put their bags in the trunk. Refusing their offers for help, the girls got into the car. Max handed Olivia the key. *"Buon Viaggio, signorine."*

"Goodbye!" the girls called out in unison.

Low and behold the engine actually started up.

As Olivia drove the car out of the parking area past the three smiling men, Greer's gaze was trapped by a pair of burning black eyes.

*"Ciao, bella."* He mouthed the words.

That place at her throat started throbbing again.

"Okay guys," she said once they'd reached the highway. "So far so good, but something tells me we'll have problems when we reach Genoa airport."

Piper's head swung around. "You're right. It's another setup to get us in their beds. The crew will alert their buddies to be waiting for us. They'll say we've stolen the pendant and the whole rigmarole will start all over again. I wouldn't be surprised if they've got a friend tailing us right now."

"Neither would I," Greer muttered. "One way or the other, they're planning on a little fun in the sun with us. Did you see those Cheshire cat grins they gave us as we were driving away?"

"Deep down they're furious the pendants turned out to be worthless."

"They're not going to leave us alone."

"It's time to call in the troops, guys."

"Tom told me they can get a flight on a military transport whenever they want," Piper informed them. "He was hinting like mad at the time."

"There's just one problem with that," Greer cautioned. "If we send for the guys, it'll be like telling them we're really interested in them."

"Maybe we *should* take our parents' advice and try to fall in love for a change," Olivia muttered wistfully.

After a minute Piper said, "We could look at this as a final test. If the boys can get here by tomorrow, we'll spend the rest of our vacation on the *Piccione* with them. By the end we'll—"

"Be dead of boredom," Greer finished for her.

"That's true," Olivia agreed, "but the crew doesn't have to know that."

Greer started to smile and sat up straighter in the seat. "You're right. Max isn't sure if there's a Don in my life or not. It would really frost him if one of the men answering to that name showed up tomorrow tossing a Frisbee around on the deck."

Piper grinned. "Especially in their military haircuts and

fatigues. They have the kind of obnoxious attitude that'll drive our crew right up a wall.''

"I love it," Olivia exclaimed, "but I guess you guys realize that if they can come, we'll have to pay Signore Moretti more money.''

"If we don't make a decision one way or the other, then we're stuck alone for nine more days with three playboys who intend to play no matter what!" Greer cried.

"Guys? Let's get serious here. I say we just get back home and back to normal. We could ring Walter Carlson and use him to run interference for us at the airport.''

"Good idea," Olivia murmured. "I see a trattoria up ahead. We can pull in there and make a credit card call.''

When they reached the parking area Greer said, "You guys stay put because we don't dare leave the car unattended. I'll talk to Mr. Carlson. It's seven-thirty in the morning in Kingston. I doubt he'll have left his house yet.''

"Let's hope your right.''

To Greer's relief it wasn't long before the wife of the owner of the busy restaurant signaled her to come behind the counter to use the phone.

Greer's fortune seemed to be holding when Mrs. Carlson said her husband was still home.

"Greer?''

"Hi, Mr. Carlson. Sorry to bother you, but this is very important.''

"I heard you girls were detained at the jail in Colorno by mistake," he said right off. "I'm so sorry, my dear.''

She blinked. "How did you know?''

"When you gave the police commissioner my name, he got in touch with the attorney for the House of Parma-Bourbon who rang me to verify who you were.

"We had a long talk about your background and the pendants your parents gave you. After he explained about the confusion over the stolen pendant from the ducal museum, he assured me he would arrange for your immediate release.''

Greer gripped the receiver tighter. ''I wish the commissioner had told *me* he was in contact with you.''

''Though I'm sure it didn't seem that way to you at the time, the Italians have a very efficient system.''

*The good old boy network you mean.* Greer almost laughed in his ear.

''Are you girls all right now?''

''Actually we're not.'' Without wasting any more time, she told him about their problems with the crew of the *Piccione*. ''We're pretty sure they're in league with one of the policemen at the airport. I'm afraid we might be prevented from boarding the plane for our flight home.''

''Don't worry, Greer. All you have to do is tell the head of security you wish to call me if there's a problem. Just mentioning my name will produce results.''

Yeah. Sure.

''Thanks, Mr. Carlson.''

''You're welcome, my dear. As I told you in my office, women weren't meant to be on their own. The attorney for the House of Parma-Bourbon agreed with me.''

Greer was counting to twenty.

''Perhaps now after this unfortunate experience, you will believe me. As I said, if you have any more trouble at all, give me a ring.''

She was about to tell him the police wouldn't allow her to call anyone, but it would be a wasted effort on her part. At this point she was so furious, she couldn't think, let alone talk. ''I will. Goodbye.''

After hanging up the receiver, she marched straight out of the restaurant to the car.

''How did it go with Mr. Carlson?''

She shot Olivia a speaking glance. ''Remember my

quote, *Don't upset me. I'm running out of places to hide the bodies?*"

"Uh-oh."

"What did he say?"

"I'm afraid we're on our own, guys."

"You mean he was no help at all?" Olivia cried.

"He said all we had to do was tell the head of security to call him if there was any trouble."

"Sure." Piper let out a defeated sigh.

Greer sat back in the seat. "Like I said, we're on our own. But I'll give you the long version of our conversation on the way to the airport."

"Your presence does us great honor, Signore di Varano."

"*Grazie,* Signore Galli."

"What can I do for you?"

Except for an obsequiousness that was irritating, there was no sign the other man seemed nervous or caught off guard by Max's unexpected appearance at the custom's area of the airport.

"The three American *signorine* you detained two days ago have just arrived at the short-term parking area of the airport in a blue Fiat."

Signore Galli's brows lifted in surprise. "I thought they were in the custody of the commissioner at Colorno."

"I'm afraid he was prevailed upon to let them go."

The other man's eyes narrowed. "It would not have happened if I had been in charge."

"I'm sure of that," Max said in an ironical tone. "Therefore I'm enlisting your help."

"Whatever I can do."

"I have reason to believe one of the Americans is attempting to take the original pendant out of the country."

His eyes screwed up. "You mean it is a different one from the three they were wearing when they arrived?"

"Confidentially, I believe they are acting as messengers for the person who stole the whole Maria-Luigia collection."

"You mean——" Max could hear the officer's mind working. "They wore the fake pendants here, then got hold of the real one to wear back?"

"Si."

"That is very clever."

"So are you, Signore Galli. You have a nose for your profession."

The other man's face warmed with pleasure.

"However I must have proof," Max added.

"Of course, signore. As soon as they reach the outer doors, my men will pick them up and escort them here. My office across the hall is at your disposal."

If Signore Galli was acting, he gave a convincing performance of total innocence.

"Grazie. Send the one with the lavender eyes to me first."

Without wasting another moment, Max entered the empty office. Once he'd closed the door, he pulled out his cell phone and rang Nic.

"Where are they now?" he asked when his cousin acknowledged.

"Lugging their suitcases through the upper level to the doors. I never saw three females so determined."

The Duchess sisters were headstrong all right. A breed of women all their own. "You'll be happy to know Galli's men are ready and waiting."

"What's your gut impression of him by now?"

Max pursed his lips. "I could be wrong, but I don't think he's involved. There was a kind of earnestness in his desire to help that didn't seem feigned, but you can never be sure."

"That is true. I'll swing the car around in front of the terminal and wait for you."

"Good. Expect us in about twenty minutes. Ciao."

While he waited, he lounged against the desk and phoned Luc who was standing by on the *Piccione.*

"How's the leg?"

"I picked up another prescription of pain killers. The pills should be working any minute now. How are the *belles mesdemoiselles?*"

"According to Nic, *obstinées comme d'habitude.*"

As both men were chuckling, he heard footsteps outside the door. "Sorry to cut this short, but our lovely jailbirds have just flown in. *A tout a l'heure, cousin.*"

"*Oui.*"

He hung up and waited with growing excitement to see the shocked look on Signorina Greer's face when she discovered him inside the room. But instead of the door opening, he heard a familiar female voice say, "Knock, knock, Signore Max. Come out, come out, wherever you are."

He opened it and glimpsed a pair of eyes that glittered like amethysts in the sunlight. But the mocking smile on that luscious mouth of hers was all he needed to see black.

"Sorry to spoil your surprise. I'm afraid the man of mystery revealed his true colors a long time ago."

"*Basta, signorina—*" Signore Galli warned in a forbidding voice. "Enough! You do not know to whom you are speaking."

The man came to Max's defense so quickly, he was convinced Fausto Galli was simply a dedicated agent doing his job.

"Of course I do! I may not have been told his real name, *signore,* but I know him very, very well. He is the shark who has been biting at my heels since I made the unfortunate mistake of swimming in these waters.

"He's the one who took me for a little roll beneath the

waves to soften me up. There's nothing he enjoys more than playing with his victim for a while first. A little nip here, a little tuck there.''

A surge of adrenaline exploded inside Max's body. "Touché, Signorina Greer— Acid-tongued and predictable as ever." He looked at Signore Galli. "Grazie. I'll handle this from here."

"Handle what?" she lashed out. "You've got us where you want us. No more games. Do your worst so we can go home."

Pleased to see she'd lost some of her cool, he smiled. "I'm glad you recognize there's no escape. Signore Galli? If you will please instruct some of your men to accompany the other *signorine* to the front of the terminal with their bags, I'll escort Signorina Greer myself."

"Of course."

Without waiting for a response from her, he picked up her suitcase, then cupped her elbow to guide her down the hall. She shook off his hand as if it had scalded her and walked ahead of him. It gave him the opportunity to watch her long, beautiful bare legs move faster and faster.

Even without a shower or fresh makeup, and still wearing the same pink skirt and top she was dressed in when she dived overboard last evening, she moved with a feminine grace that was stunning to watch.

Her sisters arrived at the Fiat first. While Nic helped them into the back seat, the security men loaded the bags in the trunk. Max opened the front door for his proud Duchesse pigeon as he'd started to think of her, then he went around and got behind the wheel.

The silence was palpable throughout the drive from the terminal to Genoa's harbor. From time to time he caught Nic's grin through the rearview mirror.

Just for the fun of it he turned on the radio to a music station that played a lot of songs in Italian and English.

As soon as he heard an old Dean Martin classic, he turned up the volume and sang along.

"When the moon heats your eye like a beg pizza pië, that's amore. When the moon starts to shine like you've had too much wine, you'll know you're in love…"

"Oh please—" the woman sitting next to him moaned before bursting into uninhibited laughter.

It was totally unexpected and it enchanted him.

*She* enchanted him.

By the time they could see Luc waving to them from the boat, her sisters' uncontrollable laughter had joined in. But his senses were only attuned to her.

"I would do more tricks for you if it would make you laugh like that again, Greer."

"A bilingual shark who *seengs* off-key. I underestimated you, *signore*. Better to hear a woman laugh than cry, eh?"

"I would never wish to make you cry."

"What *do* you wish, *signore?*"

"To help you and your sisters enjoy the rest of your vacation."

"No. You want us to help *you* enjoy *your* vacation. Admit it!"

He and Nic got out of the car and assisted their guests to that part of the pier where the boat was moored.

"I admit there is nothing we would enjoy more than to spend nine more uninterrupted days and nights in your delightful company. But you're wrong in assuming that we're on vacation."

She stood there with her arms tightly folded at her waist, not willing to step one foot on the *Piccione*. "That's right. The security guard works hard at spotting rich women for you. You work hard at relieving them of their unnecessary jewels. When you've exhausted that avenue, you work hard at seducing them. I forgot."

"You wound me again, *bellissima*."

Her head reared back, giving him an even better view of her provocative mouth. "That's another lie. I don't see a mark on you."

"The deepest ones are hidden, but we're digressing from the point."

"So there is one?" she derided.

"On the surface, Luc, Nic and I are guilty of everything you've said."

"Tell us something else we don't already know."

"Gladly, Greer. We're working undercover to find the person or persons who stole the Maria-Luigia jewelry collection from the ducal palace in Colorno. It's one of Italy's greatest treasures and the object of an intensive search that has involved the CIA, Scotland Yard, Interpol and Italy's top investigators.

"Perhaps now you can imagine that your arrival in Genoa wearing three identical Duchesse pendants, drew a collective gasp from not only Signore Galli, but the hundreds of other security people who've been involved in this case for over a year.

"If the American agents had done their part before you left Kennedy Airport, you would never have been allowed to board your plane. Needless to say, their intervention would have spared you all the unpleasantness you've been forced to suffer in the last forty-eight hours.

"From our point of view however, the Americans' lapse in security did us an inestimable favor. Though you've been cleared of any wrongdoing and are free to go—as you found out when you spoke to your attorney from the trattoria—you've unwittingly provided us with a valuable piece of information the jewel thief doesn't know about yet.

"Here is the point you were so charmingly urging me to make, Greer. We would like you to stay in Italy long enough to help us lay a trap for him, or her, or them. Whoever it is…

"You don't have to cooperate, of course. It might even be dangerous to do so, though we'll do everything in our power to protect you.

"If your answer is no, I will drive you to the airport right now and send you back to New York first class on the next plane leaving Genoa.

"If your answer is yes, we will go below for a meal and discuss our strategy in detail." His gaze took in all three of them. "The decision is yours, *signorine*."

Greer eyed her sisters, not knowing what to believe. She eventually flicked the first mate another suspicious glance. He stood there with his long powerful legs slightly apart, his hands clasped in front of him.

"If you're on the level, why didn't you just say all this at the airport in front of the head of the security?"

"Signore Galli may be one of several security people operating on the wrong side of the law. We're not certain who we can trust, perhaps not even the commissioner at the jail in Colorno. That is why we pretended to be members of the crew of the *Piccione*."

"I knew none of you were who you claimed to be," her voice grated.

"You're no captain!" Piper blurted.

"Nevertheless I have done a lot of sailing in my life, *señorita*."

"And you're no chef!" Olivia accused the man named Luc.

"*Non, mademoiselle*. But I like to cook now and then."

"If you showed us identification, we'd never know if it was fake," Greer practically hissed the words. "Are you going to tell us Signore Moretti is your superior?"

The first mate's eyes had narrowed to slits. "No. A personal friend. He lent us the car."

"*And* the boat?"

"Yes."

"Of course he did. Everybody has a friend who owns a catamaran worth close to a million dollars who just lets you take it when you want."

"You watch too many American movies, Greer."

"No—that was our mother," she snapped.

"We'd still like to see your ID," Piper insisted.

Without hesitation the men pulled out their wallets and passed them around. Greer was still staring the shark down when Olivia handed her the first one.

Nicolas de Pastrana, Marbella, Spain: six-three. Brown hair, brown eyes. Age thirty-four. Gorgeous photo.

The next one came around. Lucien de Falcon, Monacoville, Monaco. Whoa: six-two. Black hair, gray eyes. Age thirty-three. Another gorgeous photo.

Greer's hand trembled when Olivia handed her the third wallet. Maximilliano di Varona, Colorno, Italy. Maximilliano— Hah! He's six-three. Black hair, black eyes. Age thirty-four. No photo of him could be as breathtaking as the real thing.

The way European names were put together could be misleading. All of the men had a "de" or a "di" following their first names, which could mean nothing more than the fact that they were the son of so and so. Or it could be a sign they were part of an important family. Take your pick.

No doubt these exceptional male hunks had handpicked their fake names for a reason. One she and her sisters would never know about. She lifted her head and handed him back his wallet.

"I still don't believe a single word you say."

He chewed on his lower lip. "Would it help if I told you I'm chief counsel for the House of Parma-Bourbon?"

"You mean *you're* the one who had a long talk with my father's attorney? The one who affected our release from the prison?" Greer let out an angry laugh. "And would it help if I told you Piper is really the Duchess of Guasfalla, Olivia is really the Duchess of Piacenza, and I'm really the Duchess of Parma?"

"Come on, Greer," he said in a thick toned voice. "Let us put the jokes aside."

# CHAPTER NINE

"YOU know who I am."

She blinked her eyes with great exaggeration. "I do?"

"You as much as admitted it in your jail cell."

"I did?"

"You did, *mademoiselle*," Luc asserted. "Max told me and Nic all about the Husband Fund, so there's no use denying it."

Nic nodded. "The calendars are the proof, *señorita*. To be more specific, the scene in the pastry shop in Parma?"

"You mean where Violetta didn't give Luigio any of her chocolate biscotti? What does that have to do with anything?"

"They weren't the only two characters in that picture," the first mate inserted. "There was a third character recognizable due to the ducal corona emblem."

"Oh that— He was just the local pompous peacock strutting about town in his fancy duds trying to impress everyone with his family title. You know...the symbolic, typical, flamboyant Italian male, all puffed up with self-importance.

"If you took careful notice, Violetta was only toying with him to make Luigio jealous. She really adores Luigio who suffers from a private tragedy he keeps to himself. She's determined to find out what it is. Deep inside she really admires his humility. But we've gotten off the subject again."

"That's another touching story, Greer," Max said, sounding oddly violent. "I'm surprised you're not a writer."

He moved closer to her, invading that circle of space she needed to think clearly. "But you're right. We've strayed from the main line of questioning. Are you going to tell me you didn't admit to using the Husband Fund to go spouse hunting?"

"I admit it, but I still don't have a clue who *you* are."

"You mean you just picked me out of a group of candidates?"

"I might have done if you'd been lined up on the stage at a bachelor auction. For a guy who's been over the hill for thirteen years, you're still not half bad."

His hands were no longer clasped in front of him. They'd formed fists at his side. "Over the hill?"

"Yeah. After twenty-one *all* men go downhill, but as I said, you're still pretty well preserved even if you have some gray hairs at the temple. However getting back to the point *I* was trying to make before you interrupted me, I thought I saw a shark in the pool of the Splendido.

"No one could have been more surprised when I discovered it had legs and had started walking toward *moi*. If you recall, I waited until I was asked before joining you for a swim."

His features took on a chiseled cast. "So what you're saying is, you were so desperate to find a husband, you were willing to go after the first male who approached you, not knowing one thing about him? Not his name? Not his background?"

"Wow!" Her eyebrows lifted. "You sound just like Daddy. I wouldn't be surprised if you faked your age along with your name on your driver's license. Are you sure you don't have a daughter tucked away somewhere? You know—do as I say, not as I do?"

There was an uncomfortable moment of quiet before he said, "Positive."

Puzzled by his brief, quiet answer she said the next thing

that came into her head. "I knew you were a good swimmer. Does that help"

"That's important to Greer," Piper interjected. "That's how Don got her to go out with him in the first place."

"Larry had a phobic reaction to water. That's why he could never get to first base with her," Olivia explained.

"Guys— Signore Maximilliano doesn't want to hear about my love life any more than I want to hear about his."

"Then you admit that a man over the hill can still have one," he insinuated. It was a borderline sneer.

"Of course. And you've already told me about yours. It's the one thing to come out of your mouth I believe with all my heart."

His lips suddenly twitched. "When did I tell you about it?"

"You said, and I quote, 'If there's one thing I know about women, they don't feel dressed without their purse.' You certainly couldn't have made a statement like that unless you'd had prior knowledge.

"But if we could possibly tear ourselves from the riveting subject of your frantic love life, I'd like to know how you thought up such an amazing name for yourself. Obviously it was coined from the bloody days of the Circus Maximus.

"But it truly is fantastic. I mean, if there is an honest to goodness Maximilliano who's a duc or something equally pretentious running around Parma, does everyone really have to call him by his whole name?"

To her surprise, all three men exploded with laughter. The full-bodied kind that brought tears to their eyes.

"Very well, Greer," he said as soon as quiet reigned once more. "It's clear we've reached a stalemate, a term you as an American will recognize from your own courts of law. In the case of Duchess v Varano, trust is lacking on both sides of the Atlantic.''

''That was brilliant, signore. I couldn't have said it better myself.''

He gave an almost imperceptible aristocratic bow that to her surprise seemed instinctive. ''Knowing and accepting that fact, I'd like to offer a plea bargain.''

''Plea away, *signore*.''

The corner of his compelling male mouth lifted. ''We really are trying to catch a jewel thief.''

She squinted up at him. ''I can believe that. A collection of jewels falling into your hands might not make you as rich as the Count of Monte Cristo with Nic and Luc here impersonating the Count of Cabalconti and company. But you'd at least have enough to cover taxes on all the money you make under the table so to speak.''

His smile broadened. ''Good. We're making progress.''

''*Are* we. How nice.''

''Come to Monaco with us on the *Piccione*,'' he urged, his eyes focused on her mouth. ''A handful of people we've considered prime suspects will be there for the Grand Prix. With your help we might be able to flush them out.''

''We need your help,'' the captain spoke up.

''No way, Jose,'' Piper responded. ''The next thing we know we'll end up at the mercy of some potentate from outer Mongolia! Greer's right. You'd sell us to the highest bidder for profit.''

''Then I have another suggestion,'' Luc interjected. His gaze had traveled to Olivia. ''Since you are such an excellent driver, you take your sisters to Monaco in the Fiat.

''We'll sail the *Piccione* to the Port d'Hercules and join you at my apartment. That way you won't have to fear we've pirated you away to some distant shore, never to be seen or heard of again. I have to admit that would be a great tragedie.''

One look at Olivia's eyes and Greer could tell her sister was tempted. She'd dreamed of seeing the Grand Prix for years.

''It's a good plan, *signorine*.'' The so-called Max had spoken again. ''Give us tonight and tomorrow. Then we'll put you on the plane home from Nice.''

''What exactly do we have to do?'' Greer demanded.

''Just be the people you were when you came to the Riviera. We'll introduce you as the Duchesses of Kingston. There is no such English title anymore, but most people wouldn't know that, so don't change one iota of your story.'' His eyes flamed like black fires, reminding her of the first time she'd seen him at the pool. ''Wear one of those filmy, floaty concoctions I hung up in your closet.''

Her legs almost buckled from the sensuality in his tone and look. ''And the Duchesse pendants of course,'' she added.

''Of course.''

''And when we're not being used for bait, what *other* plans do you have for us?''

His elegant shrug fascinated her. ''Whatever your heart desires. A private dinner and dancing on a palace patio dripping with bougainvillea, followed by a swim in a secluded lagoon.''

Goose bumps broke out on Greer's skin. As for Olivia, her eyes were glowing a hot blue.

''Instead of swimming, I'd rather go on to a club where some of the Formula I drivers are partying and get their autographs.''

''That could be arranged Mademoiselle Olivier.''

''What about you, *señorita?*'' Nic asked Piper.

''I'd rather go to bed early, then get up at dawn and

walk around making sketches of everything for a new line of calendars I have in mind.''

"I'll prepare a picnic for us. While you draw, I'll feed you.''

"Just no olives, Spanish or otherwise.''

He threw his head back and laughed. "I promise. Only chocolate truffles and pastries. I happen to be a chocoholic myself.''

For once Greer's sisters wouldn't look at her.

They were *caving*. But who could blame them? Whoever these men really were, Greer and her sisters had no business being around them.

"Where exactly *is* this supposed apartment of yours, Monsieur Luc?''

He flashed Greer a silvery glance. "I will draw you and your sisters a map." For a man needing a cane, he got around with amazing speed and returned from the cockpit with paper and pencil in hand.

Greer could just imagine where his diabolical map would lead. Probably straight to the island castle where poor Edmond Dantes had been imprisoned.

"Don't worry, Greer,'' the dark stranger interjected. "You won't have to drive as far as Marseilles. In any case, the Château D'If is now a museum.''

Flame scorched her cheeks. He was doing it again. Reading her mind.

Luc handed Olivia the paper.

Greer smirked at Max. "X marks the spot.''

His heart-stopping smile was in evidence once more. "You may even find your ultimate treasure there.''

Her eyelids narrowed. "It's always about the treasure, isn't it, *signore*.'' She wheeled around. "Come on, guys. Let's go.''

She picked up her suitcase and started walking toward the parking area. By the time she'd reached the car, her sisters had caught up to her. Olivia opened the trunk and they stashed their bags.

"Are you mad at us?" Piper asked after they'd driven off.

"No."

"Yes, you are," Olivia gainsayed her.

"Maybe a little. But after you caught me kissing Maximus the Great in the stateroom, I have no right to point a finger."

"Even if they are a bunch of liars, we weren't exactly telling the truth ourselves when we pretended to be real duchesses. It won't hurt us to try to find Luc's house and enjoy ourselves a little before we go home."

"Come on, Olivia," Greer complained. "Do you honestly think they're going to let us near an airport before the nine days are over? Because if you do, I have a pendant in my jewelry box worth a million dollars I could sell for double that depending on the right buyer."

"Greer! What's happened to you?" Piper cried.

"Not a thing."

Olivia gave an emphatic nod of her blond head. "Yes, it has. You're different. You've been different since the night you jumped into the Splendido pool with the splendid Maximilliano. Let's face it. You finally met a man who caused you to lose your inhibitions," she reasoned.

"Now you're angry because he's the one man on earth you don't know if you can trust. Worse, after we go home, you know no other man is ever going to make you feel the same way again."

Her sisters stared at her in that pitying way she couldn't abide.

"I'm not feeling *that* bad!"

"Yes, you are."

"For someone who gets your directions confused when

you drive, it was very clever of you to notice we were sailing in the wrong direction yesterday.''

''We know how much you'd love to visit Elba and Monte Cristo.''

''Your sacrifice was heroic.''

Greer took a steadying breath. ''So was yours. I know how much you were looking forward to telling Fred and Tom you skied on the Italian and Spanish Riviera.''

''So we'll water ski some more with the guys when we get back home.''

''Yeah.''

''Yeah.''

''It'll be fun.''

''Sure it will. The Hudson Riviera.''

''At least it's safe.''

''Yeah.''

''The guys never pull any surprises. They just ski.''

''Yup.''

''They don't try to be something they're not.''

''Nope.''

''They wouldn't know how.''

''Nope.''

''They speak one language.''

''Football.''

''Yup.''

''I bet Tom doesn't know Pope Gregory was Greek.''

''He isn't Catholic.''

''Nope.''

''Fred hates Italian food. He says olive oil makes him sick.''

''Yup.''

''I bet Don's never heard of Spanish olive oil.''

''Nope.''

''It's for sure he doesn't have a clue Venus rose from the sea. He thinks it's a planet.''

"Yup."

"They're sweet."

"Yup."

"They're boring."

"Yup."

"They're looking for a wife."

"And the crew of *Piccione* are looking for a one-night stand," Greer reminded them. "I for one don't plan to give in when I don't know one thing about Maximilliano, even if that is his real name, which it probably isn't."

"But you know the chemistry's there," Olivia stated. "That's something neither of you can fake."

"So now I'm supposed to let desire take over?"

"Not completely. Just enough to wangle a marriage proposal out of him. That was the whole purpose of the Husband Fund. If you hang in there, then you won't have to pay back the $5,000 after we get home."

"Is that what you're going to do with Luc?"

"I'm thinking about it. I could always grab his cane and beat him over the head if he tries to force himself on me."

"They don't need to force themselves on women," Piper muttered. "If anything, I would imagine it's the other way around. We're probably such an anomaly, it has made them chase after us.

"But I know this momentary thrill they're feeling won't last. The second we *let* them catch us long enough to wangle a proposal out of them, they'll run so fast we won't have to dump them."

"Piper has a point," Olivia said over her shoulder. "Before we left Kingston, you were the one who reminded us we had to try hard to find a husband, Greer.

"To be honest, at this point I'd rather be wined and dined for the next twenty-four hours than have to go home and work my head off for another $5,000 only to have to give it back to Mr. Carlson."

Greer stared blindly out the back window. "Mr. Carlson's an idiot. Can you believe he actually bought all that gobbledygook about some attorney for the House of Parma-Bourbon clearing us?"

"Still, he was Daddy's attorney," Piper reminded her. "And Daddy did stipulate what the money was to be used for."

Yup. There was no way getting around that salient fact. Greer frowned to see that her sisters were ninety-nine percent won over to the idea of carrying out their original plan.

"Has it occurred to you the crew might sail off into the sunset and never be seen again?"

"No—" they both said at once.

It was a dumb question since it would never occur to Greer either. "Okay, but don't cry foul to me if we discover them waiting for us at some disreputable bar on the waterfront where they hang out with the handiest female upstairs."

"Greer!"

"Don't be so touchy, Olivia. I'm only thinking of the movies I've seen about undercover agents and their sleazy apartments."

"I think we all recognize these playboys aren't secret agents," Piper declared. "So where do we go from here?"

Olivia smiled. "Let's leave the car and the keys at the rental place. Since the crew enjoys undercover work, let them figure out where to find it."

"Yeah."

"Yeah."

Once again they found themselves driving on the outskirts of Genoa. After making several inquiries they spotted the sporting goods store pointed out to them. However there wasn't a rental bike to be had at any price.

"So we'll buy the cheapest ones they have and take them home on the plane with us."

By the time they'd purchased helmets, gloves, and water bottles they had to fill with bottled mineral water, they'd each spent $900, which they put on their company credit card. The salesguy was so happy to make an easy sale, he let them use the store bathroom to change into clean jeans, cotton sweaters and sneakers.

They helped each other put on their pendants. After stuffing their pockets with passports, tickets and wallets, they were ready. Olivia left the car parked around the side of the building in an alley with the key under the front floor mat.

Greer didn't shed any tears over their clothes and luggage sitting in the trunk. It had all been a huge mistake.

After looking at the brochure map, they estimated that if they went ten miles an hour, they could reach the town of Alessandria by nightfall. It lay in a northwesterly direction toward Switzerland where they would fly home from Geneva.

There were a dozen little stops they made to rest and snack, but on the whole they weren't unhappy with their progress. The locals waved to them from their fields and farms.

Hardly a man drove by in a car or a truck who didn't try to carry on a conversation with them and throw them kisses. They must have heard the word *"bellissima"* a thousand times if they heard it once.

Obviously Maximilliano came by his amorous ways from the same gene pool as his countrymen. So why couldn't she smile and laugh off his attention the way she did all the strangers along the road?

Halfway to their destination Piper's rear tire went flat. They took it off, then got out her patch kit to repair the tube. That's when trouble started. Every male or group of males who drove by in either direction decided to stop and help.

There must have been ten to fifteen guys young and old standing around creating a bottleneck. One truckful of guys was really pushing it. Talk about being chatted up!

Various offers were thrown out to drive them into town. Most of it was said in Italian of course, but Greer didn't need a translator to get the gist. More guys kept stopping. They were gathering like an army of ants attacking a grain field.

Then suddenly Greer saw Max's tall, powerful body striding toward her with Nic and Luc not far behind.

Like Moses parting the Red Sea, he rapped out Italian in such a forbidding fashion, the crowd of aggressive males dived for the nearest car or truck and drove off. In that instant, her heart thudded against her rib cage.

He picked up her bike with one hand like it was a toothpick. "Luc must not have drawn you an accurate map."

"On the contrary. It was marvelously detailed. A child could have found its way. However we decided the Grand Prix was overrated and thought why not see Switzerland instead to avoid the crowds."

"Since this is your first time in Europe, you had no way of knowing you can't go anywhere in summer without bumping into a crowd. Or creating one…" he added in his low, velvety voice.

"I'd like my bike back."

He'd started walking toward the Fiat with it. "All in good time, *signorina*," he announced after he'd put it in the rack on top of the car.

"You have no right to follow us and commandeer our transportation."

When his black eyes flashed right then, she felt the same authority emanating from him that had intimidated the crowd and sent his poor countrymen running for cover.

"Not only is your safety our top priority, we have a responsibility to Fabio Moretti who lent us his boat and his car for our undercover work. Though you didn't realize your Husband Fund escapade would involve you in the center of an international criminal investigation, you no longer have the luxury of throwing caution to the wind.

"If you were to meet up with some unscrupulous men who wouldn't let anything stand in the way of taking what they want, or worse…" He paused for emphasis. "Fabio could ultimately be the one held liable for something that wasn't his fault. And all because you entered into a contract with him."

He was speaking like a lawyer again.

"Since the death of his parents, Fabio has run a respectable business. He has two brothers, a wife, a child and another child on the way who depend on him for their survival."

She didn't flinch. "Don't you dare lay that guilt trip on us. How do we know you're not as unscrupulous as the men you're talking about?"

"You don't. But I can assure you that if we *had* been the kind of men you're describing, you would have been taken directly from the airport to the magistrate of the Genoese court and incarcerated in a prison for months while you awaited trial."

*Who was this man?*

"To think a female with such skin and eyes, such a beautiful body and intelligent mind as yours, has no softness in her." His gaze pierced hers. "I once suffered a great surprise and disappointment, Signorina Greer. Until now, nothing else has ever come close to it…"

Greer had to admit she was surprised at how deep the wound he'd just inflicted had penetrated. Possibly to the core of her soul.

"Where are you taking us?" she asked in a dull voice.

"To Vernazza, *signorina*, where you will sign a legal form in front of witnesses that releases Fabio Moretti from any and all obligations to you. At that time, your $12,000 will be refunded in cash, never mind that he lives hand to mouth to make ends meet and will suffer for the loss.

"But that won't be your problem will it. You'll be free to ride your bikes all over Europe and reap the whirlwind if that is your desire."

Before long the six of them were on their way back to Genoa and the *Piccione*. With Luc at the wheel, Olivia at his side, the forty miles the girls had covered in four hours only took twenty-five minutes to retrace.

Nic had pulled Piper onto his lap, which left Greer sandwiched in back between him and Max.

While the other two men tried to get her sisters to talk and acted for all the world as if nothing was out of the ordinary, Max treated Greer to a debilitating silence. It enflamed her that he'd placed the blame for the unbreachable wall of anger and mistrust between them solely at *her* feet.

But by the time they were back on the boat, the fear that he'd spoken the truth about Signore Moretti had been eating at her conscience.

"Guys? We've got to talk!" Once they'd assembled in the same stateroom, which was beginning to feel like home away from home, she unloaded on them.

After relating the thrust of her bitter conversation with Max, Piper said, "I'm not sure what's true and what isn't, but I do know one thing. None of those men who stopped to help us fix our bikes did it out of altruism. In fact that one truck load was so aggressive, I was really beginning to get nervous, you know?"

"We all were," Olivia murmured. "Let's be honest and admit we were relieved the crew showed up when they did. There's fright, and then there's fright."

Piper nodded. "With the crew, you're scared you might actually start believing all the words that come out of their mouths in half a dozen languages."

"*Liking* it you mean," Olivia amended. "With those men in the truck, you're just plain scared."

Greer's sisters had put their finger on the dilemma plaguing her since the night Max had asked her to swim with him. He *could* have behaved exactly like those men in the truck. Because of her instant and overwhelming attraction to him, she would have been helpless to deny him anything for long.

But he'd let her go. Not once, but three times. The last being in the jail cell. He'd known how vulnerable she was last night, both physically and emotionally, yet he hadn't taken advantage of her or the situation.

Like a revelation it came to her that his actions weren't those of a despicable brute who preyed on defenseless women. But they *were* the actions of a man searching for answers, determined to find them.

Though Greer didn't know who he was, or what he did for a living, the close call on the road this evening showed her the situation for what it was.

Whether he was a jewel thief or not, seduction was the last thing on his mind. The pendant had been the catalyst to bring them together.

If there really was another pendant like the one their dad had given them, and it had been stolen along with a priceless jewelry collection, no wonder alarm bells had sounded when she and her siblings had waltzed through customs wearing "hot" merchandise.

At this juncture Greer was prepared to believe that once the crew had accomplished their business in Monaco, they would put her and her sisters on a plane home.

Familiar vibrations caused her feet and legs to tingle, alerting her they'd cast off. "Guys? I'll be right back!"

To her sisters' astonishment, she dashed out of the state-room and through the hall to the upper deck.

Genoa, the bejeweled lady of the Mediterranean, was receding in the darkness which had enveloped the coast without her being aware of it. Greer could still make out Luc's physique as he coiled rope.

She turned her head to discover Max securing the bikes next to the kayaks. If he felt her presence, he didn't acknowledge it until she'd come within touching distance of him. Then he lifted his dark head and their gazes collided.

His anger had dissipated, but in its place she sensed a new aloofness emanating from him. It was the kind he might show any stranger rather the woman he'd kissed with unbridled passion two days ago.

If anything she should be relieved by this seemingly professional detachment. It was what she wanted. Yet her mouth had gone strangely dry and her heart was behaving like a single engine plane spiraling out of control as it hurtled toward the ground coming up to meet it.

"Whatever you wish to say, tell it to the captain, *signorina*. He pilots this boat, not me."

Her awareness of him made it difficult to breathe.

"But he listens to his first mate. Please inform him that we're going to spend the next few hours transforming ourselves into the Duchesses of Kingston.

"After we've reached Monaco, we plan to make such a stunning entrance, even *you* will blink and wonder if you've been wrong about our not having a drop of royal blood in us whether it be Austrian, Italian or something else."

# CHAPTER TEN

"Oh...you guys..." Olivia's voice shook with emotion. "Just look at that sight..."

It was a Monagasque fairyland all right, with the Grimaldi royal palace glowing like the crowning star on the Christmas tree.

From the balcony of the gorgeous villa overlooking the street where the Formula I cars would race tomorrow, Greer and her sisters feasted their eyes on elegant old palaces and buildings with wrought-iron railings, wonderful roofs with thousands of orange tiles laid at all angles in multifaceted splendor. There was a veritable panoply of painted walls, architectural detail, friezes, scrollwork everywhere one gazed.

Farther below lay Monaco's fabulous harbor twinkling with lights from the myriad of small white boats including the *Piccione* and stately yachts the size of soccer fields. Possessions of the world's wealthiest princes and sheiks.

Piper sucked in her breath. "I'm looking and I still don't believe it. Smell the flowers. They're everywhere. Jasmine and rose. Lavender."

It was the stuff dreams were made of all right, Greer mused in awe. Yet this nineteenth-century provencal villa named Le Clos des Falcons was breathtakingly real.

So was the black limo with its royal falcon crest which had whisked them and the crew from the port. Where others couldn't go, they were allowed entrance past barricades, guard rails, fences and gates erected for the world's most famous car race.

Olivia nudged Greer in the ribs. "What do you think of Luc's sleazy waterfront pad now?"

"Obviously he has friends in very high places."

"It feels like we're in a beautiful dream."

Greer smiled at her sisters. No doubt she was walking around the sumptuously furnished room wearing their same, starry-eyed expressions.

"If mother could see us in our knee-length white chiffon and pendants, that's exactly what she'd say."

Piper stared at Greer. "We look like identical triplets tonight. It really shows since we're wearing the same hairdos for a change. Wouldn't she love it? Mom always begged us to dress alike on special family occasions."

"I can hear Daddy now," Greer murmured. "Are these my three darling duchesses all grown up?"

Olivia's eyes went teary. That started Piper and Greer. Everything was still blurry when she heard a distinct rap on the outer door of their private suite.

Assuming it was the maid who'd been waiting on them since their arrival, Greer went to answer it, unprepared for the sight that awaited her.

There stood the heartthrob of the century. No doubt about it. Max would win the prize hands down.

He probably heard the moan that escaped her throat, but she couldn't help it. In black and white formal evening wear, this tall, black-haired Italian with his striking aquiline features left her speechless and trembling.

His black eyes roved over her in male admiration. Yet the fire she'd always seen burning in their depths when he looked at her was missing. Extinguished if you like.

Greer didn't like, which was absurd. This man didn't mean anything to her. He was an experience. A phenomenon of nature like the planet Mars coming close to Earth for the first time in sixty thousand years, then continuing its orbit to the far reaches of space.

Tomorrow night Greer's plane would follow its own orbit to another part of the universe. The chance of their ever coming together again, even for an instant, wasn't astronomically possible.

"*Buona sera, signorina.* In five minutes we'd like you and your sisters to come down the staircase at the end of the hall. There's a drawing room off to the right where you'll be introduced to a group of people. Just play along with the conversation wherever it leads."

She got a sinking feeling in the pit of her stomach. "What if we make a mistake?"

"You won't if you just play at being your unique self which you do superbly."

The acid comment was meant to wound. It found its mark.

"When the time comes for the guests to withdraw to the dining room for a midnight supper, I'll make our apologies and we'll both leave. At which time I will say goodnight."

Greer shivered because beneath his civility she sensed he was still furiously angry with her.

"As for *you, signorina*, you look exceptionally beautiful tonight. Since you will have served your purpose for us with the grace of Violetta herself, you'll be left alone to do whatever you want. The limo's at your disposal. Just tell the maid and she'll arrange it."

"We heard that," Olivia whispered after the door closed in front of Greer's face. "I take back what I said. He's scarier than any man I ever met."

"We shouldn't have bought those bikes," Piper murmured. "I think it insulted him. Maybe it's an Italian thing. You know what they say about travel in a foreign country. In some places it's polite to burp after you eat, in other places it isn't."

"Baloney!" Greer spun around. "It's a *male* thing. He

didn't get his way the minute he snapped his fingers, so now he's having an Italian temper tantrum.''

"I think you're having one, too. Your face is all splotchy. It proves we do have some Italian blood in us despite the mean things they said to try to discredit us.''

"Thanks, Olivia.''

"Don't bite my head off. We know you're disappointed.''

"About what?''

"About his intention to leave you strictly alone after we've done our part downstairs,'' Piper murmured.

"I couldn't care less.''

"That's not what your eyes are saying. But don't worry. I'm going up to bed right after, too.''

"So am I.''

Greer's gaze shot to Olivia's. "I thought Luc had arranged for you to visit a club to meet some Formula I drivers.''

"That's out of the question now.''

"Why?''

"When I told him Cesar Villon was the only driver I was interested in meeting, he demanded to know why. I asked why he cared. He didn't answer, but his whole mood darkened after that.''

"Sounds like he's as jealous as Fred,'' Piper reasoned.

"No. He's just an egocentric French male who thinks the world begins and ends with him. You know how the French are. His eyelids go all hooded.'' She imitated him, laying on the French accent. "He becomes the melancholy philosopher's philosopher. He's seen it all, done it all, and he knows it better and has suffered it longer than anyone else.''

Whoa, Olivia!

"The captain's the one who *knows* it all,'' Piper insisted. "He's got what I call the Castilian superiority complex. You can't say one thing that he doesn't know more about it, and he's *the* authority. There is no other above him. In his spare time he makes up Spanish crossword puzzles of the highest difficulty.''

"Did he tell you that?" Olivia questioned with a chuckle.

"Not yet. I'm waiting. It has to be on his resume somewhere.''

"Piper!" Greer was laughing, too.

"Do you know he thinks I'm a chocoholic? So of course that's what I am, right?''

"All three of us are," Olivia muttered.

"Never mind that. It's what *he* thinks and says I am, I can't abide. You can't win an argument with him. It's impossible. He's always one step ahead of you. That Spanish brain is like a steel trap, stored with obscure trivia he pulls out at a moment's notice.

"He thinks he's spending tomorrow morning with me so he can impress me with more of his vast knowledge." Her cheeks glowed a hot red. "Get this— He says I'm the only American woman he ever met who can converse with him on a halfway intelligent level.

"Well guess what? This dimwit American has gathered enough of her scattered brain not to go anywhere with him in the morning or any other time.''

"You won't say that after you've spent five minutes with him again," Greer reminded her, "but let's not worry about that right now. It's time to go downstairs and do what it is we're supposed to do.''

"I still don't know what that is," Olivia complained.

"You heard Maximilliano." She loved to say the name, wondering if it really was his. "Just play ourselves.''

"I think that was meant to be an insult.''

Greer glared at Piper. "You only *think?*''

They made their way through the villa, which felt more

like a palace. There was a striking man in elegant evening clothes waiting at the bottom of the curving staircase. When he smiled up at them, Greer realized it was the owner of the *Piccione*!

What was going on? The girls recognized him immediately and rolled their eyes at Greer.

"*Buona sera, signorine.* You were lovely before. Tonight you take my breath away."

Anger over this whole charade emboldened Greer to say, "You look pretty smashing yourself, Signore Moretti."

He flashed her a smile that could have meant anything.

*Sure* he was just a poor catamaran owner... One furthermore living hand to mouth who would be held liable if anything happened to the lovely *signorine*.

The man had a great thing going here. If there really was a Signora Moretti and child, Greer felt sorry for them.

"When the other party had to cancel their reservation for the *Piccione* at the time of the Grand Prix, it became your lucky day, did it not?"

"The experience of a lifetime," Piper said through gritted teeth.

Olivia's hand went to her throat in a dramatic gesture. "We still haven't recovered. It's like we're moving through an amazing dream."

Nightmare you mean.

He chuckled. "I'm very happy to hear it. Shall we go in? I'll introduce you to a few guests." He opened one of the ornate floor to ceiling doors.

Greer blinked. A few people? She'd been aware of chamber music, but not voices. There had to be at least seventy beautifully dressed guests congregated in groups around the elaborate appointments of the drawing room! If the crew was there, she couldn't tell.

"Fabio!"

An attractive dark blond woman wearing a stunning oyster toned designer dress, left the people she'd been talking to and hurried across the parquet floor with her handsome escort to kiss Signore Moretti on either cheek.

The other man, evidently her husband, stood a few inches taller than Fabio with enough gray in his black hair to make him distinguished. Both looked to be in their early sixties.

A spate of Italian broke from all three of them, giving Greer the impression they were close friends who hadn't met for a while. But then nothing about this trip had been as it seemed. What was the line, "We are all actors and the world is our stage"?

"Rina? Umberto?" Fabio spoke up. "There are three sisters I want you to meet," he explained in English. "They chartered the *Piccione* for this time slot. When I found out who they were, I decided to keep it a surprise until tonight."

"So much alike, yet the eyes are so different." The woman smiled warmly as she and the other man studied each of them. Then her dark flashing gaze that put Greer in mind of the great black's, suddenly locked on the pendants. She let out a cry that brought her husband's arm around her shoulders. All conversation in the room ceased.

With a chuckle Fabio said, "No, Rina. You and Umberto are not hallucinating. May I present Greer, Piper and Olivia. They are the Duchesses of Kingston of the royal House of Parma-Bourbon, anxious to meet their long lost family."

His announcement created a shock wave of interest throughout the crowd.

"Because of the theft of the Maria-Luigia jewelry collection, there was some unpleasantness when the *signorine* came through customs a few days ago wearing the Duchesse pendants.

"You will be happy to know it is all cleared up now.

Signore Rossi has determined that one of the pendants they're wearing is the other original made by Tocelli for Maria-Luigia.''

"Other?'' The word echoed throughout the room as everyone looked at them in astonishment.

"For some reason yet to be uncovered, the artisan fashioned two identical pendants. Therefore it appears that the myth about an ancestral line making its way to America is not a myth after all.''

What? But the crew said—

"*Signorine?* May I present your many distant relatives. First of all, Rina and Umberto, the Duc di Varano of the House of Parma-Bourbon.''

Greer and her sisters let out a collective gasp that was even louder than the cry of the other woman, the woman they'd just been introduced to who could be none other than Max's *mother!* The resemblance to both parents was unmistakable.

But that meant the first mate was the son of a d—

"Come, *signorine.*'' Fabio started ushering them around the room. "Meet your hosts for this evening, Violetta di Varano, Umberto's sister who is the wife of Jean-Louis, the Duc de Falcon of the House of Bourbon.''

Another duc? Luc's mother was named Violetta?

*Noooooo.*

Olivia's groan coincided with hers. Luc's parents smiled broadly. "An exquisite surprise,'' his father murmured before kissing their hands with the kind of dashing charm bequeathed to their injured son.

Greer was still reeling with shock and rage, unable to take it all in.

"Standing next to them is Maria di Varano, the second sister of Umberto who is married to Juan-Carlos, the Duc de Pastrana of the House of Bourbon.''

"What a thrilling moment for the Varano family,'' Nic's

mother responded with genuine pleasure. "Niccolo will have to sort all of this out for us. He's the expert in the family."

A hysterical laugh emerged from Piper's throat. Thankfully Fabio continued to sweep them along, making the introductions of the rest of the guests, one of whom could possibly be the person responsible for the theft of the ducal palace jewelry collection. Undoubtedly Signore Moretti was watching everyone's reactions, which he would report to the crew.

There was no sign of *them* yet.

It was a blessing, particularly since she suspected her sisters were on the verge of strangling someone with their bare hands. Greer would be the first in line, and she knew which neck she wanted to start with.

The three of them drew close together for a second.

Olivia drew in a noisy breath. "Luc de Falcon is going to wish he didn't need a cane because when I get hold of i—"

*"Signorine?"* came Fabio's voice. "Last but not least, may I present Isabella di Varano, wife of Giovanni di Luccesi—"

*"And my only sister."*

Of course.

The grand entrance of Maximilliano the Magnificent himself!

"This is very exciting," the dark-haired beauty exclaimed.

Isabella was as gorgeous as her brother, but Greer refused to look at him.

She couldn't fathom any of what was going on. In truth she was only barely functioning.

"If all of you will excuse our bellissima Duchesse cousins," Max spoke in a vibrant voice that would have penetrated the farthest corners of the room. "They need their rest after spending a miserable night in the Colorno jail while I worked out the legalities with the police.''

The crowd's sympathetic reaction couldn't possibly have been orchestrated.

''Following their release they chose to take a grueling four-hour bike ride in the hot sun to see the countryside of their ancestors. Unfortunately they ran into some trouble that required my help again.''

Greer stole a look to see if he'd been struck by lightning yet. What a horrible mistake that turned out to be. His black eyes were *laughing* at her.

''I'm quite sure they're at the point of exhaustion, but as the chief commissioner confided to me, they charmed the guards and handled their harrowing ordeal with all the dignity and spirit of the former Duchesse of Parma herself. *Signorine?* May I be the first to say, welcome to the family.''

His mockery in front of God and all these witnesses who were clapping after such an amazing speech was too much.

''Thank you,'' Greer said to everyone with a smile. ''It's been a pleasure to meet everyone.'' Her sisters said virtually the same thing before they all murmured their good-nights.

She made her exit out the door with the kind of poise her parents would have been proud of. The girls weren't far behind. After reaching the foyer, they flew up the staircase to their suite like a bunch of homing pigeons.

Once the door was locked Greer turned to her sisters hot-faced. ''We know we're not related, so how *dare* he mock us like that. Now that we finally know which way the wind is blowing, we'll see who has the last laugh.

''No way are they going to get the satisfaction of bundling us up in the royal limo and shipping us back to America like so much unwanted baggage. Obviously that was their plan as soon as they were through using us.''

Olivia wore a set jaw. "We came to see the Grand Prix and that's what we're going to do."

"We can escape off the balcony," Piper muttered. "It'll be a cinch. I saw a little portico just below it. From there we can jump to the ground and merge into the crowd before they discover we're gone."

Greer marched over to her suitcase. "This operation calls for jeans and T-shirts, but we'll have to be wearing our travel suits when we ring for maid service."

Within a few minutes several of them appeared at the door to carry the luggage to the limo.

"Thank you. We'll be right down."

The second the door was closed, they peeled off their suits, hung them in the closet, then put on their casual clothes and sneakers.

They met at the balcony. "One for all, and all for one," Piper whispered before going over the railing first. It was like déjà vu, except that instead of water, they landed on pavement.

Piper was off like a shot between two villas across the street. Olivia followed close behind. Greer brought up the tail as they discovered a narrow alley farther on and started running like crazy in the direction of the harbor below.

The crowds of spectators waiting all night to see the race roamed the streets and alleyways, impeding their progress. But it no longer mattered because she and her siblings blended with the crowd.

Farther down when they came out on the main street again, they passed a set of bleachers with a huge "Villon" banner fastened across the top. Olivia stopped in her tracks. "You guys—"

"We know. We saw it, too."

"Let's find out if there's room for three more."

Whether it was because they were triplets, or because the gods were smiling on them, a group of exuberant

French guys probably in their late teens and early twenties seemed only too happy to let them squeeze in next to them.

They spoke little English which made it amusing. In every other way they communicated like mad. Olivia's knowledge of Cesar Villon's racing statistics enamored her to them. Greer and Piper just smiled and pretended they were hard-core fans, too.

For the first time since the girls' arrival in Europe, they were treated like royalty. The one named Simon fed them ham filled brioches. The other ones named Gerard, Jules and Philippe, supplied drinks and treats. They carried pocket transistors that picked up all the information about the drivers and the cars. Excitement ran high.

Then came the first rays of the sun and with it the roar of the race. Screaming engines permeated all of Monaco, loud, close, far and soft. Between the unintelligible reporting of the announcer over the loudspeakers plus the echo of the cars bouncing off the buildings and hills, the thrill of the sport was like a fever in the blood.

Fans dotted the scene before them like bits of pepper in a pasta dish. Some were draped over balconies, others hung out of windows, still others looked through the holes in fences all along the route. When Cesar Villon roared by, there was an explosion of noise that probably broke a few eardrums.

Greer looked over at Olivia who was being hugged by one of the guys in the excitement of the moment. She nudged Piper who put her lips to her ear so she could hear her. "Seeing Villon whiz by has made this trip for our sister."

"I'm glad one of us can go home with a good memory." Greer's temper was still as hot as a firecracker.

"When do you want to head for that youth hostel Simon told us about. I'm ready to pass out from lack of sleep."

"You're not the only one. Let's go."

They called to Olivia who nodded and started making her way toward them. The guys tried to talk the three of them into staying. The only way Olivia could persuade Gerard to let her go was to tell him to come by the hostel that evening. By then they'd be ready to party.

"He drew me a map, guys," she said as soon as she reached the aisle of the bleachers. "With this crowd it's about an hour's walk from here."

"After yesterday's bike ride, it'll be a piece of cake."

Max instructed the helicopter pilot to fly over the *Piccione* again. Since it had been determined that their prize pigeons had flown off the villa balcony while he and his cousins had been picking Fabio's brains for information about the guests' reactions to the news, there'd been no trace of them. Not at the Nice airport, not at the train station.

"Every police officer had been given a description and was told to call in at the first sign of them. Where in the hell could they have gotten to so fast without being detected?"

His cell phone rang. It was Nic who'd been working with the police on the ground. "Did you find them?"

"No. We've checked with the concierge of every hotel. There's been no report of seeing them at the reception counters. They haven't asked for a room. What about the boat?"

"Fabio says they haven't stepped foot on it," Max muttered.

*"Dios!"* Nic thundered.

None of them wanted to entertain the thought that the women had been so desperate to get away from them, they'd asked a lift from some predators who had no interest in racing and only came to Monaco for just such an opp—

"Hang on, Nic. Luc's calling." He put him on hold and clicked to Luc. "Any news?"

"They're seven blocks from the villa!"

*"What?"* His heart practically leaped out of his chest.

"I just saw them on the TV screen while a cameraman was panning the lower portion of the route chatting with fans. They're being very cozy with a bunch of enamored college guys sitting on some bleachers bearing a Villon banner.

"Mon Dieu— I don't know where my mind has been not to think of that first! The stand is next to the corner of the Rue de Cypres. If I didn't have this damn leg holding me back—"

"You *have* your leg! That's the most important thing, and it's going to get better. Because of you, we now know where our pigeons have come to roost. Nic'll round them up. In the meantime I'll instruct the pilot to fly over the area so I can keep an eye on them. I'll call you back as soon as I know anything more."

He hung up, gave the pilot new instructions, then clicked on to Nic and told him the situation.

"I'm on my way now with the police," his cousin responded with a noise in his throat that sounded oddly emotional to Max. Was it possible Nic was coming back to life after all these months?

Max waited till the helicopter had reached the desired vicinity. Using his binoculars, he zeroed in on the stand in question, but he didn't see the face he was looking for. No hair of spun gold. The knowledge that the women had already fled the scene hit him like a kick in the gut.

"Keep circling," he rapped out to the pilot while he waited for Nic to arrive. In a few more minutes his cousin approached in a police car, followed by two more patrol vans. He and half a dozen officers got out and started interrogating everyone on the bleachers. It seemed to go on a long time.

Eventually he noticed four of the spectators being escorted to the vans. Good. They knew something!

Before long Max received the call he'd been waiting for. "Nic?"

"The women have gone to a local youth hostel on the Avenue Prince Pierre."

Unbelievable.

"Our witnesses refused to cooperate until we threatened them with a night in jail for obstruction of justice. No doubt they were planning to meet them there later for a few nights on the road together," his voice grated.

Max ground his teeth so hard, pain shot through his jaw. "How much lead time do we have on them?"

"Probably forty minutes."

"It's enough for Luc to set things up the way we want. I'll meet you back at the villa."

After clicking off, he phoned Luc and let him know what was happening.

"Leave it all to me, Max. By the time you both get here, we'll be able to relax and catch some sleep before tonight."

Sleep? What was that?

Since the moment he'd followed Signorina Greer inside the San Giorgio church in Portofino where he'd first glimpsed her face in the candlelight, he'd felt an unprecedented stirring in his blood.

The sight of her distinctive profile, the texture of her skin giving off a glow of natural pearls, those violet orbs—all had kept his legs planted in the shadows where he could feast his eyes on her without detection.

She had a lovely body. In the flattering sundress, she was the essence of classic femininity. The kind that would grow more beautiful when she became a mother.

Haunted by that image, he'd left the church ahead of her, hungry and restless for the one thing in life that would always elude him.

"Max?"

"Yes?"

"Are you all right?"

"Of course."

"If you say so, *mon ami*." There was a click as he replaced the receiver.

# CHAPTER ELEVEN

"WE DON'T have individual rooms, *mesdemoiselles*. Our dorms have four bunk beds each, eight people to a room. Right now we only have four beds left in the whole center."

"Is it an all women's dorm?"

The receptionist at the Centre de Jeunesse Pierre shook her head. "We don't make distinctions here."

Of course not.

Greer turned to her sisters. "I don't think I can go on without some sleep."

"I can't, either," Piper murmured. "You can bet these are the only four beds available in Monaco."

"I don't see we have a choice, guys," Olivia declared.

"Agreed." Greer pulled out her wallet and handed the receptionist the credit card. At the rate they were spending money, there would be no profit to bank at the end of the year.

So far they were out their designer luggage, their wardrobes, their bikes and $15,000 they would have to give back to Mr. Carlson. If it hadn't been for the generosity of Simon and the boys, they would have been forced to buy breakfast, too.

The woman handed them three sets of clean sheets, blankets and pillows. "You're in dorms four, five and six upstairs."

They wouldn't even be in the same room. "Thank you."

At the top of the stairs they paid a visit to the rest room before moving on to the dorms. To their relief, each one was empty. Naturally no backpackers would be hanging around here. Not while the most exciting event in the world's most romantic spot was happening right outside the building.

All the bottom bunks had already been claimed by other guests. Olivia looked around her dorm. "If our luck holds, no one will show up until tonight. By then we'll have had our sleep and can head for the train station."

"Let's set our watch alarms for 7:00 p.m. That'll give us a good few hours to recuperate."

They hugged Olivia goodnight, then went to their separate dorms. Somehow Greer found the strength to climb up the ladder and fix her bed before collapsing on top of it. Yet five minutes later she was still awake.

Max's last words to the guests in the drawing room kept running through her mind. *Welcome to the family.*

His mockery, meant as the final affront before he put her on the plane home from Nice had been particularly hurtful.

Greer knew why... She was in love for the first and only time in her life.

Hot tears gushed from her eyes. She buried her face in the pillow. It was a good thing her sisters weren't in the room. They'd never seen her cry over a man before. And they never would!

When next she became cognizant of her alarm going off, she was so out of it she rolled off the mattress to get up like she usually did, then screamed to feel herself falling.

"Oh!" she cried out again when a pair of strong masculine arms caught her before she went splat on the floor.

"Easy, *signorina.*"

"*Max!*"

She blinked several times while she tried to figure out

if she was awake or dreaming. Right now the black eyes staring into hers at such close range were alive with flame.

"How did you find me? What are you doing here?" She was so in love with him and so cross with him at the same time she couldn't see straight. "Where are all the other people?"

"What other people? Don't I even merit a 'grazie' for saving your life?" he whispered against her lips, nibbling them as if they were delicious morsels he couldn't resist.

She groaned because he was kindling the ache that had never gone away since he'd first kissed her. Rivulets of desire coursed through her body which yearned toward his. She was trembling with needs he'd brought to life, needs that would never go away.

"Put me down first and we'll talk about it," she begged in a breathless voice. This close to him she couldn't think.

His mouth roamed over her face, her nose, her eyes, her hair. "I can't do that, *bellissima*. I've learned that the only way to get anywhere with you is to keep you in my arms. I want you, Greer. I want you with a hunger you couldn't possibly comprehend."

His mouth was doing the most incredible things to her. In his arms she was learning the meaning of rapture. When they got tangled up with each other on the narrow lower bunk, she couldn't tell where one kiss ended and the next one began.

Ecstasy. That's what it was like being kissed by Maximilliano di Varano. Ecstasy.

Her fingers twined in his raven-black hair and she found herself covering his face and throat with her mouth, savoring everything male about him while she worshipped the differences between them.

"You were right to call me a shark," he whispered huskily as he caressed her throat with his lips. "I'd like to take bites out of you in order to make you a part of me.

"But if I did that, then you would be consumed, and I would go mad with hunger because there wasn't any more of you, anywhere. Let me take you back to the *Piccione* where we can be alone and I can love all of you," he begged with primitive longing.

Back to the *Piccione*? For only one night?

In that moment her heart dried up like winter's last prune.

Deliberately misunderstanding him, she leaned over him, pressing his cheeks with her palms. Pain like she'd never known before intensified the purple glow of her eyes.

"You've made me so happy, I'm frightened. Do you think you could talk Fabio into letting us take the *Piccione* on a long, long honeymoon? I want to go to Elba, Monte Cristo and a hundred other islands with you. I want to experience everything with you.

"You've set me on fire, and now I'm the one bursting from the love I want to shower on you. I want to be all things to you. I want to live with you night and day.

"I want to have your babies," she cried against the male mouth that had transformed her. "Beautiful, brilliant, wonderful babies just like their father.

"You won't be doomed to swim forever alone, searching for me but never finding me. Once we're married, you can make love to me whenever you want. Whenever I want. Whenever we both want, for the rest of our lives if we want. How does that sound to you, my darling?

"You are my darling you know," she kissed the corner of his mouth, the lashes of his eyes, the lobes of his ears. "Don't you know a hundred lifetimes from now I will love you even more than I love you right now?

"Yet I can't imagine it being any stronger than it is at this very instant. There's no man who comes close to you,

Max. I love you. I love you to the depth of my soul.'' Her voice throbbed.

"I honestly didn't know love could make me feel like this. I didn't realize," she whispered, her breathing shallow. "Kiss me again so I'll know this is real."

She sought his mouth once more with soaring passion. "I can't wait to be your wife. I realize we haven't known each other very long, but it doesn't matter. Not when you've found your soul mate."

Staring into the black depths of his eyes she said, "We *are* soul mates. I knew it when you asked me to guess your name, knowing such a task would have been impossible. It was the most thrilling moment for me because I knew you wanted the experience to go on and on and never be over.

"I wanted it to go on and on, too. More than anything in my life I wanted to swim in the moonlight with you. But my feelings were too intense that night, too raw. I felt like one of those white-hot stars out in space ready to implode. Oh Max, I—''

"Greer—" he spoke her name in a gravelly voice, shifting her aside so he could get to his feet.

His breathing sounded ragged. The broad chest beneath the cream knit shirt he was wearing rose and fell visibly, like he'd just run a marathon. She'd terrified him.

That was the prophecy she'd made to her sisters months ago. It had come true. She knew he would run once he thought marriage was on the cards. But it hurt with a pain from which she would never, ever recover.

She slid off the bottom bunk. "What's wrong, darling?"

He rubbed the back of his neck with his hand. His face was a study in agony. She had no idea he could look that way.

"I forgot I was dealing with a woman who has obviously never been to bed with a man before."

Really. Her inexperience stuck out that badly? She'd thought her wild response to him was probably more uninhibited and reckless than any initiated woman he'd ever made love to before.

"No," she answered in a bright tone. "I haven't. I've never had the slightest inclination until I saw you get out of that pool and come walking toward me as if you wanted to devour me. Since then I haven't been able to think about anything else but marrying you and making love with you for the rest of our lives."

After a long, palpable silence, "Greer—" he said her name again. The ultimate playboy of the Riviera seemed to be choking on monosyllables. It had to be a first for him, so why wasn't she jumping up and down with glee?

He raked a hand through his hair. "I'm afraid taking you out to the *Piccione* isn't going to work after all."

He'd finally been able to spit out the words, but they emerged sounding like a tormented whisper. How weird!

With the entire female population throwing themselves at him from every direction, why was it causing him such upheaval? Why such suffering to deny himself the pleasure of a one-night stand with a virginal American from the wrong side of the tracks?

"What do you mean?" she cried out in spurious alarm.

When he didn't say anything else, she decided it was time to help him out.

"Why don't you just admit you would love to make love to me, but not if it means getting hitched first!"

"Greer—"

She laughed. If her sisters had been present, they would have called it her cruel laugh.

"Take it easy, Max. It's not the end of the world. You're off the hook. You always have been."

His dark head reared back, exposing his hard jaw. "Explain that remark."

Putting her hands in her back pockets, she smiled up at him. "I'll be happy to. At the jail when I was telling you about the Husband Fund, I'm afraid so many other matters were discussed at the same time, I left out the most important part."

"Which part?" he demanded in a chilly tone.

Greer cocked her head to the side. "This'll take a few minutes. Would you like to sit down first?"

Like a magnificent colossus, he remained standing there.

"Fine. Have it your way." She flashed him another sunny smile. "My sisters and I never worried about getting married, but our parents did."

His scowl was quite frightening. "We've been over this ground before."

"True, but there's more. Unfortunately you have to be patient because I'm a woman, and you know how women are. They have to lay everything out and build up to it, analyze it, discuss it, and dissect it to death before they get to the point.

"It's just one of the great differences between the sexes men have so much problem with. Especially a man like you."

His mouth thinned. It delighted her, even if the withered prune which had been her heart was dissolving fast.

"As I was saying, our parents were concerned enough about the situation that during Mr. Carlson's reading of a letter our father had written to us, Daddy asked us to watch a movie about these ladies who try to find millionaires to marry."

"I've seen it," he interjected in a low voice.

"Of course you have. Anyway, the whole idea was to put ideas in our head to find a rich man and settle down.

"The film was a complete turnoff."

She paused. "You're pacing. Why don't you sit down? I told you this would take a while."

If looks could kill. "Go on."

"The loss of both our parents who needed constant nursing care over a couple of years was harder on us than we thought. After Daddy died, we moved across the street to a basement apartment so the house could be sold to pay the bills. I guess we didn't see that we needed a break until our landlady suggested to Piper we could use a vacation.

"But you know how it is when you're a workaholic, because that's what we are. We loved college, love our work and find it much more stimulating than anything else we do.

"So...until Mrs. Weyland brought up the idea of a vacation, we really hadn't entertained the thought. But with $15,000 suddenly in hand, it sounded kind of fun to go somewhere exciting. If only the money didn't have to be used to find a husband which none of us wanted.

"That's when Olivia reminded us we were the Duchesses of Kingston, so why not pretend *we* were the millionaires and see how many men we could get to propose?

"Piper picked up from there and said why not wear the Duchesse pendants to bring the really hard-core playboys out of the woodwork?

"Both their ideas were brilliant. At that point I merely suggested that we vacation on the Riviera if we wanted to hit the jackpot. When any of those phony playboys actually did propose, they would disappear back into the woodwork as soon as we told them we were the poor Duchesses from Kingston, New York, with no titles, no money, no lands.

"Then we could go home as free as the air to breathe having had a fabulous time visiting the home of our ancestor and maybe picking up new markets for our calendar business."

By now Max's eyes resembled shards of black ice. He

shifted his weight, making her aware of his intimidating height. "So if I had proposed—"

"If you *had* proposed fair and square, I would have told you the truth about myself knowing you would bail."

"Which was exactly what you wanted to happen."

Ah hah. His Italian ego had been dented again.

"I thought I'd already made that clear. But to reiterate, yes! That's exactly what we wanted to happen. Don't you see? We would have obeyed Daddy's stipulation to try and find a husband.

"Could we help it if in the end our eager suitors took back their proposals when they realized there was no gold at the end of the rainbow?"

She flashed him her diabolical smile. "I certainly didn't have to worry about you though, did I. Maximilliano di Varano baled ahead of time because you don't need to force a woman to have her, and you're not stupid. Otherwise you wouldn't be chief counsel for the House of Parma-Bourbon even if you are the son of a duc."

"Grazie, *signorina*," came his brittle reply. She could envision him making that slight little aristocratic bow.

"You're welcome." Her brows lifted. "You want to know something really ironic? We even planned our scheme so that on the last night of our trip when we unmasked ourselves, we would arrange to do it at a youth hostel just to prove our point.

"I had no idea it would be this one, though. Our original plan was to end up on the Spanish Riviera where we would lure our opportunistic playboys to a hostel, the last place they would think where we were staying.

"Unfortunately nothing went the way we expected and I was denied the fun of telling one of those losers, 'Sorry. No money. No tiara. What? You mean you're taking back your proposal? Well don't go away mad. Just go away.'"

His expression had darkened as if there'd been a total

eclipse of the sun. "What if one of those...losers hadn't bailed?"

She laughed. "The kind of men we planned to target were safe bets. But wearing the pendants threw a monkey wrench in the works. Are you familiar with that expression?

"I can see that you are," she said when there was no answer. "The point is, we never did have a chance to meet a real playboy. All we've met up with so far is the good old boy network. Its members don't count."

"So there's an age?"

"Absolutely."

"How old's Don?"

Don. Again?

"He's the right age, but he's not a playboy. He's a fine man who wants to marry me and have a family. Six little boys who will all grow up to be football players."

"What's wrong with that?"

"Not a thing if you love football, which I don't mind. Sometimes it can be pretty exciting. But I'd prefer not to be looked at as a breeder."

"Breeder?"

"So—there *is* one vagary about American English you haven't run into yet. You have no idea how pleased I am to hear that. Piper complains that Nic claims to know everything about everything."

"You were saying?" he reminded her in a gruff tone.

"I was *saying* that I would prefer to be looked upon as a woman first. Complete. Total, in and of myself! I mean, what if I couldn't have children? Would that suddenly make me less desirable in his eyes? And even if I could turn out a football team for Don, what if they were girls instead of boys? Heaven forbid! Who would watch the football games with him in his old age?"

One of Max's black brows dipped. "A minute ago you

told me you wanted to give me wonderful, brilliant babies like their father.''

"That was different. You were kissing me and telling me you wanted me with a hunger beyond comprehension. You had no expectations except to enjoy me like a piece of chocolate. I liked that. You weren't looking at me as the mother of creation.''

His eyes narrowed on her face. "But you admit you'd like to be a mother one day.''

"Well, yes. One day. Of course by the time I'm ready to get married, I'll probably end up with someone who's been divorced and has children of his own.''

"I thought you wanted to marry *me*.''

"I do,'' she said honestly, "but I also have brains in my head, and eyes that can see you're not for sale at any price. Otherwise you would have married a woman of your own station and breeding years ago.''

"You're right. There's a reason why I didn't.''

"I'm sure it was good one,'' Greer asserted. "Tragedy is no respecter of persons.''

"Tragedy?''

"Yes. You're the one who said some wounds weren't visible. I got the impression you were trying to tell me something. You truly are Signore Mysterioso.

"However there are things about you I *do* know. For one thing you're not a man who plays around with other women while your wife is home trying desperately hard to pretend it doesn't bother her.

"For another, you don't take advantage of foolish virgins. On the contrary, you rush about saving them from a fate worse than death while they're trying to make an escape on their bicycles.

"Furthermore, I don't think you're the type to carry on with married women behind their husbands' backs. You don't need to when every eligible maiden in Parma would sell her soul to be *the* woman in your life.

"All in all I think you're quite a rarity, Signore di Varano. For a man that is. And now it's time for me to go find my sisters. We have a plane to catch."

He shook his handsome hand. "Not quite yet. By now they're aboard the *Piccione* waiting for you."

"For such an honorable man I must say it was very cruel of you to welcome us to the family in front of your parents and relatives after Signore Moretti told that lie about our pendants. For that I will never forgive you." But really she just couldn't forgive him for not loving her.

"Careful, *signorina*—sometimes all is not as it seems."

"Meaning what?" she grumbled.

"I'll let Nic tell you this evening while we enjoy our meal on deck."

"And then will you give us our freedom?"

"I will do better than that. When the celebration is over, I swear an oath on the graves of your beloved parents I'll take you wherever you wish to go."

She didn't think the mention of her mother and father was a subject Max would bring up if he weren't being sincere.

"Very well then. I'm ready."

He opened the door of the dorm and escorted her down the hall to the stairs. "Do you know one of the many things I find fascinating about you is your ability to travel light?"

"Normally I don't," she said as they left the hostel. He helped her into his car parked around the side.

After they'd driven off he turned to her. "The point is, you're adaptable."

"I am when I'm running for my life."

His deep chuckle resonated to the tips of her toes. "That was some disappearing act you did off the balcony."

''Did the three of you tape our escape and then watch reruns until you'd decided we'd had enough sleep?''

''No, *signorina*. We waited in the limousine to spirit you back to the boat for a midnight supper.''

She couldn't help laughing at that admission. ''Which Luc prepared of course.''

''Actually it was Marcel, one of their chefs who wasn't very happy no one showed up to eat his masterpiece.''

Uh-oh. ''How did you find us?''

''Luc saw you on TV enjoying yourselves with a bunch of hormone-riddled fans. They were so taken with you, Nic had to get the police to threaten them with jail time before they would admit where you'd gone.''

''You're kidding! They were very nice to us.''

''That's only natural since they expected to join up with you tonight for more fun and excitement.''

She bit her lip. ''They fed us breakfast.''

He gave her that wounded look again. ''All along, my cousins and I have been prepared to see to your needs.''

''Unfortunately we didn't know until a little while ago that we weren't going to be served up as the main course to fill *your* needs.''

His rich male laughter filled the interior.

''Whose idea was it to serve us petrified bread in the Colorno jail? Remember you are under oath, counselor.''

''That was different.''

If all traces of Greer's heart hadn't disappeared, his grin would have made it flip-flop as they wound their way to the port. Everywhere she looked, the rich and famous were dancing the night away to music coming from the dozens of nearby yachts and boats.

Monaco was in full party gala. So was the festive deck of the *Piccione*. The boat sat sheltered beneath one of the many blue canopies. She discovered her sisters and Max's cousins sat eating with an unexpected dark-haired guest who bore a superficial resemblance to Luc.

When Max introduced her, the man who appeared to be in his midtwenties got up to shake her hand.

"Greer Duchess, meet my younger cousin, Cesar. You will know him as Cesar Villon."

Villon? Her gaze flitted to Olivia's in confusion.

"He's Luc's younger brother," her sister murmured, looking completely dazed.

"The race car driver—" Greer cried softly. That meant—

*"Oui, mademoiselle."*

"But if your last name's Falcon?"

"It is, but Villon is another family name I use on the track." He exuded the same devilish charm of all the Falcon men.

"I see. My sister is a great fan of yours. It's a thrill to meet you. We saw you whiz by the stand early this morning. How did you fare in the race over all?"

"I came in second."

"That's fantastic. Congratulations."

*"Merci.* At first I was not happy about it, but since Luc introduced me to your sister, I have discovered all is not lost. She wanted to wait until you arrived, but now that you are here, we're going to move on to a club where a party is being held in my honor. I would like it very much if you joined us."

"Perhaps later, Cesar," Max answered for her. "Right now Signorina Greer and I have a little celebrating of our own to do."

"Ah oui?"

Everyone's gaze swerved to Max. Greer couldn't imagine what he was talking about, but when she turned to him, he was staring pointedly at Nic. "Did you tell them yet?"

"No. As Cesar said, we were waiting for you."

"We're here now." Max helped Greer to a place next to Piper, then he sat down next to her, keeping his arm around the back of her deck chair. She could feel his heat through the material of her T-shirt. It melted her insides till they ran like butter.

Nic's Castilian white smile gleamed in the candlelight. Luc's dashing features on the other hand were as somber and remote as she'd ever seen them.

"Señoritas, when Fabio Moretti announced that one of you was wearing an original pendant like the one in the Maria-Luigia collection that is missing, it wasn't a lie to smoke out the thief."

Her sisters gasped, but Greer jerked her head around to stare at her host for verification.

"It's true," Max claimed. "Therefore, it's entirely possible that you *are* our distant cousins. In time Nic will solve that particular mystery. For the present we intend to catch the people responsible for the theft. That's one of the reasons why I said welcome to the family. But there *is* one more."

Suddenly he grasped her hand so that everyone could see. His actions caused a pounding in her chest that almost knocked her off the chair.

"As I told Greer the other day, life plays strange tricks. Once a long time ago it played a bad one on me. Then very recently, while I was defending a court case in the House of Lords, life played a good trick when I received a phone call from Signore Galli at Genoa airport.

"To make a long story short, it brought Greer Duchess into my life. I knew I loved her the moment I first laid eyes on her in the San Giorgio church."

He was *there?*

"But I wasn't sure she would have me if she knew I couldn't give her children. An old soccer injury put my spleen out of commission and that was that."

Greer's breath caught, but she couldn't stop the tears that welled in her eyes for the disappointment he'd had to suffer knowing he couldn't father children.

"Tonight she took away my fear and asked me to be her husband."

"Greer!" Her sisters sounded ecstatic.

"I hope that's a sign of approval," he kept talking, "because I'd like everyone here to know I've accepted her proposal."

*Max—*

"No details have been worked out yet. No date has been set. We need the rest of the vacation on board the *Piccione* to get to know each other. To my knowledge we haven't even shared a meal together."

His gaze swerved to her sisters. "Since your parents aren't here, do I have your permission to marry her? I know this must come as an enormous shock."

Olivia shook her head. "No, it doesn't."

"Not at all," Piper concurred. "We knew it was a fait accompli when we caught her kissing you in the stateroom."

"She just doesn't do things like that," Olivia confided.

"The minute we heard she dived into the Splendido pool to join you, we realized our plan had worked and it was only a matter of time."

Greer froze in place. "What do you mean *your* plan worked?"

"Who do you think gave Daddy the idea for the Husband Fund?" Olivia said.

"Until you caved first, there was never any hope for us. Since you've always been the cautious one, we decided something drastic had to be done."

"You're kidding! You mean from the very beginning, you let me believ—"

"If everyone will excuse us," Max interrupted, pulling

her straight out of the chair into his arms. "I'd like to take my fiancée below and make this official."

When they reached the stairs he crushed her against him, kissing her passionately. "You know I love you," he whispered against her lips. "I wanted you for my wife when I first saw you in the church. My life would be nothing without you, Greer."

"Now you tell me," she teased. "But since you've demanded so nicely..."

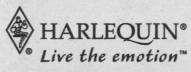

Like a phantom in the night comes
a new promotion from

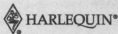
**HARLEQUIN®**

# INTRIGUE®

GOTHIC ROMANCE

Beginning in August 2004, we offer you
a classic blend of chilling suspense and
electrifying romance, starting with….

## A DANGEROUS INHERITANCE
### LEONA KARR

And don't miss a spine-tingling Eclipse tale each month!

**September 2004**
## MIDNIGHT ISLAND SANCTUARY
### SUSAN PETERSON

**October 2004**
## THE LEGACY OF CROFT CASTLE
### JEAN BARRETT

**November 2004**
## THE MAN FROM FALCON RIDGE
### RITA HERRON

**December 2004**
## EDEN'S SHADOW
### JENNA RYAN

*Available wherever Harlequin books are sold.*
**www.eHarlequin.com**                    HIECLIPSE

# eHARLEQUIN.com

### The Ultimate Destination for Women's Fiction

Visit eHarlequin.com's Bookstore today
for today's most popular books at great prices.

- An extensive selection of romance books by top authors!
- Choose our convenient "bill me" option. No credit card required.
- New releases, Themed Collections and hard-to-find backlist.
- A sneak peek at upcoming books.
- Check out book excerpts, book summaries and Reader Recommendations from other members and post your own too.
- Find out what everybody's reading in Bestsellers.
- Save BIG with everyday discounts and exclusive online offers!
- Our Category Legend will help you select reading that's exactly right for you!
- Visit our Bargain Outlet often for huge savings and special offers!
- Sweepstakes offers. Enter for your chance to win special prizes, autographed books and more.

**Your purchases are 100%
guaranteed—so shop online
at www.eHarlequin.com today!**

INTBB104

If you enjoyed what you just read,
then we've got an offer you can't resist!

# Take 2 bestselling love stories FREE!

# Plus get a FREE surprise gift!

Do you like stories that get *up close* and *personal*?
Do you long to be loved *truly, madly, deeply...*?

If you're looking for emotionally intense, tantalizingly
tender love stories, stop searching and start reading

# *Harlequin Romance*®

You'll find authors who'll leave you breathless, including:

## *Liz Fielding*
Winner of the 2001 RITA Award for
**Best Traditional Romance**
*(The Best Man and the Bridesmaid)*

## *Day Leclaire*
*USA Today* bestselling author

## *Leigh Michaels*
Bestselling author with 30 million
copies of her books sold worldwide

## *Renee Roszel*
*USA Today* bestselling author

## *Margaret Way*
Australian star with 80 novels to her credit

## *Sophie Weston*
A fresh British voice and a hot talent!

*Don't miss their latest novels, coming soon!*